Linda,
You'll love this Zeke
Layne story!
Cheers from Catawba!
Tins Up!

12/7/21

Memory Layne

The *Emerson Moore* Adventures by Bob Adamov

- *Rainbow's End* Released October 2002
- *Pierce the Veil* Released May 2004
- *When Rainbows Walk* Released June 2005
- *Promised Land* Released July 2006
- *The Other Side of Hell* Released June 2008
- *Tan Lines* Released June 2010
- *Sandustee* Released March 2013
- *Zenobia* Released May 2014
- *Missing* Released April 2015
- *Golden Torpedo* Released July 2017
- *Chincoteague Calm* Released April 2018
- *Flight* Released May 2019
- *Assateague Dark* Released May 2020

Next *Emerson Moore* Adventure:
- *Sunset Blues*

Memory Layne

Bob Adamov

Packard Island Publishing

Wooster, Ohio

2021

www.packardislandpublishing.com

www.BobAdamov.com

This book is a work of fiction. Names, characters, places and incidents are either products of the author's imagination or are used fictitiously. Any resemblance to actual events, locales or persons, living or dead, is entirely coincidental.

First edition • May 2021

ISBN: 978-0-578-86293-4

Library of Congress Number: 2021903457

Printed and bound in the United States of America

Cover art by: Ryan Sigler
Blue River Digital
303 Towerview Dr.
Columbia City, IN 46725
www.blueriverd.com

Printed by:
Bookmasters, Inc.
PO Box 388
Ashland, OH 44805
www.Bookmasters.com

Layout design by: Ryan Sigler
Blue River Digital
303 Towerview Dr.
Columbia City, IN 46725
www.blueriverd.com

Published by:
Packard Island Publishing
3025 Evergreen Drive
Wooster, OH 44691
www.packardislandpublishing.com

Dedication

This book is dedicated to the owners of the Miller Boat Line – Billy, Julene, and Scott Market in recognition of their ongoing commitment and community involvement for South Bass Island's residents and visitors.

It is also dedicated to Matt Parker, who retired as the Catawba Island dockmaster, and to my ornery Aunt Donna Goodwill as well as my loving wife, Cathy, and sweet stepdaughter, Michelle.

They that wait upon the Lord shall renew their strength;
they shall mount up with wings as eagles;
they shall run, and not be weary;
and they shall walk, and not faint.

– Isaiah 40:31

Acknowledgements

For technical assistance, I'd like to express my appreciation to Billy Market, Julene Market, Scott Market, Matt Parker, Kim Bartish, John Wisse, Jerry Davenport, Doreen Chester and Randal Lowry.

I'd like to thank my team of editors: Cathy Adamov, John Wisse, Peggy Parker, and Michelle Marchese.

Thank you to Donna Schoonmaker for suggesting the title Memory Layne. It was just so perfect!

I've had several family members and friends, who have experienced Alzheimer's, and I've observed them go through the stages. At times, it was funny as I watched them do some of the strange things like my uncle calling the police to report his car as being stolen after walking out of the barber shop and not seeing the car parked to the left of the door. He had forgot that he parked to the right of the door. There have also been the scenes that are so sad. I acknowledge them for inspiring me to capture some of their moments in Memory Layne.

For more information, check these sites:
www.BobAdamov.com
www.VisitPut-in-Bay.com
www.MillerFerry.com

Lake Erie Islands

MEMORY LAYNE

CHAPTER 1

Miller Ferry Dock
Catawba Peninsula, Ohio

The rhythmic sound of Lake Erie's waves splashing the rocks below the worn wooden deck reminded Zeke Layne of his once strong heartbeat, but he wasn't going to complain that it skipped beats now. He had a good life for the eighty years he already had lived.

He watched as a number of seagulls gracefully skimmed the water, searching for prey. Several swooped down in daring dives to seize their unsuspecting targets, then beat the air with their white wings as they departed with their catch firmly gripped in their beaks.

Adjusting his black-framed glasses, Layne leaned forward while seated in his faded, blue deck chair. He squinted his tired eyes to focus through the early morning mist across the South Passage toward South Bass Island. There was no sign of the Miller Boat Line ferry.

There was a bite in the late August breeze coming across Lake Erie's western basin that morning, and Layne was glad that he had slipped on a worn, dark blue jacket. It had the Miller Boat Line name lettered in white. He wouldn't have to wear it very long. The sun's summer rays soon would warm the day and he could discard it before he headed to the dock to follow his daily routine.

Under the jacket, he wore a blue denim work shirt and dark blue Dickies cotton twill work pants. He didn't wear a belt. Those days were long gone. His rotund belly caused a daily battle with gravity. His pants kept slipping down. He resolved his ongoing struggle by wearing a pair of bright red suspenders. It helped in spotting him whenever he wandered away, which occurred more often as the Alzheimer's disease advanced.

As he sipped his coffee, he thought back to his preretirement days as a ferry boat captain for the Miller Boat Line, running passengers, vehicles and freight from the Catawba Peninsula to the Lime Kiln dock on the island's south side. Those were fun-packed days, especially on days when the storms blew in and the waves heightened to challenge his skill at the helm.

Then there were the late November days when the temperatures dropped and sleeting rain caused an icy sheen on the ferry's deck, sending vehicles and passengers sliding about. Those days, he didn't miss. The cold weather bothered him more, he noticed as he aged.

He had the resigned look of someone who realized that he was slowing down. His cardiologist recently advised that his heart needed a stent, but the procedure could be dangerous. Layne previously suffered two heart attacks that had weakened his heart and didn't want to take a chance, although his daughter urged him to have the surgery.

His memory was failing. He previously had been diagnosed as being in the early stages of Alzheimer's. That worried him more than the heart problem. He noticed that he was becoming more forgetful. He was getting lost, misplacing things and forgetting appointments, but some of those he did on purpose.

People teased him as they tried to determine if he was using his forgetfulness to his advantage. And, at times, he did.

His thinning, white hair was offset by a thick, white beard that did little to hide his ready smile. He was known for his infectious and impish smile – one that radiated warmth, kindness and calm. He was quick to smile and crack a joke or offer a compliment, especially to a pretty lady. His eye lines would crinkle up like his forehead when he laughed or showed affection.

His wizened face was highlighted by his thick, white eyebrows and large, black-framed glasses that did little to hide his blue eyes. His captivating eyes lured people into his stories as they wondered if they were just tall tales being spun.

He had a slight tremor in both of his hands and he joked that he could make a milkshake by holding a glass filled with ice cream and milk if he held it for three minutes. His back was slightly hunched and his head would bob at times.

Dropping his hand to the side of his chair, he rubbed the head of his golden Lab. Sheba responded with a cheerful bark and licked his hand. She had been his companion since his second wife's death ten years earlier. Layne found her next to the road after she had been struck by a car and he rescued her.

Sheba followed him wherever he went and was no bother, other than one bad habit she frequently displayed. She couldn't help herself. She would bolt at the sight of a rabbit and disappear, but always returned home to his side.

As he stroked her head, he noticed that a spider had built a cobweb below his deck railing. The rays of the morning sun glistened off the morning dew on the spiderweb.

He looked down at his patient dog. "Sheba, do you want to play fetch?"

The dog barked as she arose to her feet. She loved the morning routine, but like her master, she readily felt the effects of aging. In her dutifulness, she looked back expectantly as she saw Layne get to his feet.

He had a rubber ball in his hand which he had extracted from his jacket pocket. As he arched his back and tossed the ball into the lake below, he commanded Sheba to "fetch!" She entered the water for a short swim, retrieved the ball and confidently returned it to Layne.

"Good girl," Layne said. He patted her head and took the ball from her.

Sheba watched Layne closely. Layne threw the ball out three more times and she brought it back to him each time. When she emerged from the lake water the final time, she shook herself to shed the water from her coat before returning the ball to Layne.

Layne took the ball and returned it to his pocket as Sheba found a sunny spot on the deck and laid down. Picking up his cup, Layne slowly walked into his home and displayed a slight smile.

His lakefront residence was a 1972 mobile home which was fifty-seven-feet long and ten-feet wide. It had two bedrooms and one bath. He and his first wife, Leona, purchased it in 1990. They had a crane lift it and set it on steel pilings over the rocks next to the Miller Ferry's Catawba gift store, the Waterline. Zoning laws were more flexible back then. It would never have been permitted today.

Behind it, he and some friends built the wooden deck over the rocks with stairs descending to the rocks and a small sandy beach. His daughter had planted sunflowers along the west end side of the trailer where they stood proud and tall in the breeze. The home sat back fifteen feet from the road and had parking for two vehicles — his daughter's Chevy Cruz and his rusty 1955 Chevy pickup truck.

Layne had worked the Miller ferry since he was a teen and was close to the Market family who owned the ferry. Siblings Julene, Billy and Scott inherited the ferry business when their parents, Bill and Mary Ann, passed away. It had been Bill who had given Layne permission to set that trailer over the rocks and next to the gift store.

Layne walked into the living room, closing the door behind him. His once cluttered home was more cluttered now and so was his life. His quiet solitude had been interrupted when the two redheads became squatters. His daughter, Cathy, and seventeen-year-old granddaughter, Michelle, had moved in two years ago and shared the bedroom behind the kitchen. Cathy struggled through a difficult divorce in Cleveland that left her virtually penniless. She had nowhere to turn, but to him – and he took them in.

He dearly loved his daughter. She reminded him of his first wife Leona with her looks and her loving nature.

Chaos filled his home and his mind. Dirty clothes and stuff were everywhere. The bathroom was another story. He couldn't figure out why women needed so much stuff in the bathroom. Makeup, hair spray, blow dryers and feminine products seem to take any available free space. Several times, he noticed that his razor was on the edge of the bathtub and he knew that he didn't use his razor when he showered because he rarely used it.

And worst of all, the ladies would get on him about leaving the toilet seat up. It was his home and if he wanted to leave the seat up, he could, he argued. Besides, he always waited until the last minute and would have to rush to the bathroom. Taking time to raise the seat could make the difference between the front of his pants being wet or dry. Accidents were happening more often as he aged and his condition progressed.

Layne ambled through the living room to the kitchen and placed his coffee cup in the sink that was already filled with dishes. The countertop was also cluttered with plates, pans and grocery bags. Layne opened a bag of rye bread with caraway seeds and popped two slices in the toaster. He walked the short distance to the fridge and retrieved a container of butter. Placing the butter on the counter, he picked up a bag of dog food and poured some into a dog bowl.

He didn't fill it all the way to the top. He didn't fill anything to the top. It was too dangerous. His shaking hands would cause the contents to spill all over. The telltale coffee stains on his pants and the beige carpeting served as a visible reminder of what happened if he filled his coffee cup to the top. He placed the dog food bag on the counter and carried the half-filled bowl outside to the deck.

"Here Sheba," he said as he set the bowl next to her. "I got you some vittles." Sheba barked softly and began to chow down.

Layne returned inside to the kitchen and waited for his toast. When the toast was ready, he applied the butter and quickly downed the two slices. After he finished, he then headed down the narrow hallway to the small bathroom to brush his teeth.

Layne opened the medicine cabinet and looked carefully for his daily pill dispenser which contained his daytime prescription medications. He opened the compartment marked with a M, for Mondays, and withdrew two pills that controlled his high blood pressure and two additional pills that were prescribed for his high cholesterol. After he downed the four pills together, he walked to his bedroom and grabbed his blue baseball cap with

Miller Boat Line etched in white letters above the brim.

He paused to look reverently at the picture of his first wife, Leona, which was positioned atop his dresser. It was something he did each morning. Her radiant blue eyes stared up at him from a sweet face framed by her flaming red hair. He missed her. He missed her a lot. Cancer had taken her twenty-five years ago.

He thought back to when he had first met her. He was in his twenties and a tanned and lean deckhand on the ferry crew. Leona was in her early twenties and was spending her summer on Catawba at her parents' cottage. He met her when she slipped and fell on the ferry deck and he raced over to help her.

When their hands touched, it was as if an electrical charge raced through both of them. It was love at first sight. They had chatted briefly as she rode the ferry to South Bass Island and again on her return trip later that day.

The next thing he knew, he was driving over to the cottage to meet her parents and spend time with her. It was a quick romance as they fell deeply in love. They were married that fall. She was as fresh as the morning breeze off the lake.

He didn't display a picture of his second wife, Alva, on the dresser. That marriage had been a mistake. He was sixty at the time and Alva was forty-five. He should have listened to his friends when they warned him that she was putting on an act for him. Alva was a fake and a gold digger.

He should have known better, but he went ahead and violated one of his rules. He liked women who dressed modestly, but could get all dolled up when she was with her man. He had met Alva, a divorcee, when she and three of her girlfriends from Toledo boarded the ferry. She was wearing tight short shorts and a low-cut top that did little to cover her ample bosom. His crewmates later teased him that he was dumbstruck by her outfit.

Alva had made a beeline for him when the ferry left the Catawba dock. She sashayed her hips over to him and leaned into him as she peppered him with questions about Put-in-Bay. When she returned on the ferry later that day, she and her girl-friends were trying to recover from overindulging in alcohol. She spotted him on board and hung all over him on the trip back to Catawba.

He made the mistake of telling her that he was a widower and pointing out his trailer next to the gift store on Catawba. She began stalking him and repeatedly would show up unan-nounced at his home where she seduced him. He allowed her affectionate attention to weaken him and agreed to marry her when she pushed it.

They were married nineteen years ago. She had put on an act to catch him and discarded it a month into the marriage. It was a classic bait and switch move. She stopped cooking and taking care of the home. She began throwing temper tantrums and became very belligerent. Layne put it off to the heavy drink-ing that she did and tried to peacefully co-exist with her. She had been a whirling dervish, causing him stress that he didn't need and trying to get her hands on his savings. He blamed her for causing his heart problem.

One summer night three years ago, she stormed out of the trailer with a bottle of whiskey. She walked briskly to the end of the Catawba dock where she finished the bottle. The next morning, Layne went to find her. He found the empty whiskey bottle at the end of the dock, but no Alva. His friends helped him search for her on Catawba Peninsula, but no one could lo-cate her. He thought she had just run off and began to reconcile himself with that assumption.

Two days later, two fishermen found her body washed up on

the shore of nearby Mouse Island. The coroner's report showed that she had an extremely high level of alcohol in her. It was assumed that she had become drunk and fell into the lake where she drowned.

Alva did leave him with a legacy. An unpleasant one — her twin devil daughters, Blair and Ida. He had nicknames for them – Liver Lips and Frostbite. The two cold-hearted, scarecrow-thin women were in their thirties, had badly bleached hair and bulbous noses that drifted to the right. Their skin was as rough as a gravel beach. They were as evil as their mother, couldn't catch a man and seemed to be always after his savings – just like their mother.

They were so mean to his daughter Cathy that he compared them to the two wicked stepdaughters in Cinderella. He'd mock the two stepdaughters and tease his daughter by saying, "Sweep the steps. Clean the cellar. My dear Cinderella." Cathy didn't think it was funny.

Layne was glad that Liver Lips and Frostbite lived in Toledo. The distance helped keep them away even though it was only a forty-minute drive. The only time they visited was when they needed money, but Cathy had grown skilled at helping him repel their requests.

Turning away from Leona's photo, he left his bedroom. As he walked back down the hallway, he thought about waking Cathy and Michelle. He then decided against it. Cathy probably had worked late at the Catawba Inn, which was across the Miller ferry parking lot. Michelle liked to sleep in, and it wouldn't be too long and school would be starting up. No more sleeping in for Michelle, he thought quietly to himself.

He slowly walked into the kitchen and out the front door, calling for Sheba, who ran around the trailer to follow him. It was his daily routine. He'd walk along Water Street past his old truck and Cathy's Chevy Cruz, the gift shop and the ferry ticket booth down to the passenger shelter house where he'd spend about four hours greeting and entertaining waiting ferry passengers with his tall tales.

The passenger shelter house was a white block, one-story structure with a blue steel roof. Roll-up aluminum windows could be opened or closed depending upon the weather. There was a bench through the center of the room and more were scattered throughout. The waiting area provided vast views of Lake Erie and its symphony of wave action, passing boats, flying seagulls and the arriving and departing Miller ferries.

On the other side of the waiting area was the crew quarters, a building for the dock crew and several golf carts that the crew would use between the dock and the freight depot, which was located south of Water Street.

As he walked by the white-painted ticket booth, he saw the smiling face of one of his favorite people, Jayne Kerwin. "Morning, Jayne," he called.

"Don't you look as handsome as ever," Jayne replied. She flashed her large smile at Layne.

"I'll never look as good as you, Jayne."

He loved throwing compliments at pretty women. He felt it was easy to get away with seeing as how he was a senior citizen.

The blast of the ferry horn announced its arrival and the dock crew scurried over to direct the unloading of the first run of the day. The vehicles would drive off first, followed by any motorcycles, bicycles and passengers. They'd stream up the hill to pick up Water Street or Route 53, or to one of the many parking lots on top.

As Layne walked past the ticket booth with Sheba at his

side, he noticed a woman struggling with two children. "Can I help you?" he inquired.

"Are you catching the ferry?" she asked as she looked at the friendly man.

"No, but I'm heading that way," Layne said. He pointed to the covered waiting area. "I can give you a hand."

"Tommy Long, you listen to me," she scolded her brash four-year-old. "You walk in front of me with this nice gentleman."

Tommy stopped fighting with his sister and looked at Layne. He wasn't sure about walking with him.

Layne held out his hand. "Here you go, son. You walk with me and I'll let you play with Sheba when we get down there." Layne pulled out Sheba's ball from his pocket. "You can play fetch with her."

The boy's face erupted in a wide grin and he quickly grasped Layne's hand. "Okay," the lad said. He walked quietly with Layne to the passenger waiting area.

When they arrived, Layne took a seat near the entranceway and handed the boy the ball. The boy quickly started playing fetch with Sheba.

"Thank you so much," the grateful mother said. She watched the youngster and felt pleased.

"It's nothing," Layne acknowledged. He reached into his other pocket and withdrew a harmonica that he placed against his lips. He then began playing a tune to entertain the waiting passengers. He smiled when a number of children gathered around him like the Pied Piper.

He entertained the waiting passengers by playing *When the Saints Go Marching In*, *What a Wonderful World*, *Hotel California*, *Ring of Fire* and *We Are Champions*. He stopped playing and encouraged them to clap as he began to play *We Will Rock You.*

He liked it when passengers would break out dancing as he played *Achy Breaky Heart.* When an attractive twenty-year-old woman walked by, he'd switch songs and play *It Ain't Me Babe.* They usually stopped and gave Layne a big smile. He winked at them. Nothing like a smile from a pretty woman to make your day, Layne felt. Layne's memory never missed a beat when it came to remembering songs to play.

When a voice on the overhead speaker announced the boarding instructions for the ferry, Layne stopped playing. He stood from his seat and watched as the vehicles began driving onto the ferry. He then waved as the passengers left the waiting area and walked to the ferry.

"Have a great time," he shouted to them. One little girl stopped and turned. She raised her hand to her mouth and blew Layne a kiss. Layne's face broke into a wide smile and he blew her a kiss in return. He enjoyed his daily pastime and waiting passengers couldn't help but like the entertaining retiree.

Every thirty minutes a ferry would arrive and unload, then reload for the return trip to South Bass Island. Layne would entertain the waiting passengers with his harmonica and tall tales. He usually followed the same routine each day from 9:00 a.m. until 2:00 p.m. unless it rained. It wasn't that the rain bothered him. It was because the number of tourists to the island dropped on rainy days.

The large blast from the ferry boat horn announced its arrival. It interrupted the relatively quiet August morning that had otherwise been filled with the shrieks of seagulls and the conversations of the waiting passengers.

"Now, where was I?" Zeke Layne asked to no one in particular. He absentmindedly patted his shirt pocket to make sure that his harmonica was still tucked away. His hands reached up to adjust his stained cap on his head as he looked at the eager children standing in line waiting to board.

"Who would like to know something about the ferry boat?" Layne beckoned. "Do I see any raised hands?"

He did and one little boy shouted out, "Tell us about the ferry boat engines!"

"The engines, why of course young man. That ferry is the *Mary Ann Market*. She's the biggest in the fleet. She's got two diesel-powered engines and is about eighty-feet long."

"Mister, is that the one you drove?" a seven-year-old girl asked as she interrupted him.

He turned his head to look at her. "No. My ferry boat was smaller."

"Did you have to drive it in bad weather?" another young girl asked.

Layne nodded his head. "I did. It can get bad in November when you get freezing rain and ice forms on the deck."

"I bet you put salt on the deck to melt the ice," an older boy offered.

"No. Not salt. We'd use sand, and that didn't keep the cars from sliding around. You'd see them crash into each other," he explained.

"Like the dodgem bumper cars at Cedar Point," a wide-eyed girl suggested as she thought about the nearby amusement park.

"You are very right. Just like those bumper cars," Layne agreed.

A middle-aged man interrupted the discussion. "Are there any casinos on South Bass Island?"

Layne turned to look at the man. "No. You'd have to go to Toledo or Cleveland for a casino. But back in the 40's, the ferry boats had slot machines onboard. You could play them on the ride over," Layne explained.

Before he could continue his stories, the overhead speakers announced the boarding procedures.

"You'll be boarding soon, kids," he said. Layne pointed to the blue and white ferry that had just eased up to the dock. It began to drop its front ramp to rest on the dock. "Watch now and you'll see the cars drive off first, then the passengers will disembark."

"Do we go on next?" the girl asked eagerly.

Layne pointed over his shoulder to the two lanes filled with waiting vehicles. "They have to drive those cars on first, then they'll let you board. If you can get on board fast, you can climb the stairs to the second deck and sit right there below the pilot house. Next to being at the wheel of the ferry, that's the best seat," Layne said as he pointed to the top of the ferry. "And do you know what's really fun to watch from up there?"

"What?"

"You look down to the bow of the ferry. That's the front end," he explained. "On a day like today there's a good chance that you'll get some big waves breaking over the bow. The first-timers will be standing in the bow and they don't know that they'll get drenched."

The girl giggled.

"It's fun to watch them," Layne grinned as he gave her a conspiratorial look.

"We're going to get that seat," the girl whispered to her younger brother who had been standing next to her. She turned back to Layne. "Thank you for telling us your stories and playing your harmonica for us, Captain."

"That's what I do, young lady," Layne replied. His weathered, tanned face broke into a smile. He looked the part of someone who had spent years working on the ferry boat. His eyes were distinctive. The blue sparkled like diamonds and signaled his mischievous nature. He loved to pull pranks on people and it was a part of his Irish nature. So was his legendary drinking.

On the other side of the passenger shelter, a red-haired woman approached Matt Parker, the Catawba dock manager who had been born on South Bass Island. The tall, blond with gold-framed eyeglasses and a smile was easy to spot with his wide brimmed hat as he supervised the dock crew.

"Matt" she called as she walked over to him.

"Hi Cathy. Beautiful day."

"It is," she agreed. "Have you seen my dad?"

"He's sitting over there. Entertaining the passengers."

"Is he causing any trouble?"

Parker laughed. "Of course, he is. He wouldn't be him unless he was."

"What did he do this time?"

"He's pulled out his wallet and shows people his picture on his driver's license, then asks if they've seen the guy in the picture. They always gave him the strangest looks," Parker chuckled.

"I hope he's not a bother."

"Never. He's been such a fixture here. He can get away with just about anything. He's such a likeable guy."

"You're sure it's not because of the beer he brings down on Friday nights, right?" She knew that her father carried a twelve pack of beer down to the dock for the guys to enjoy after the last ferry departed.

"Oh never!" Parker said with raised eyebrows. He turned to supervise the vehicles driving onto the ferry.

"I better rescue your passengers," she said. Cathy then turned and walked toward her father. "Dad! Do you hear me?" she shouted, while approaching her father.

Straightening, Layne turned. "Yeah. Yeah. I hear you. What is it?"

"The doctor's office just called."

"So?" he asked. Layne ran his hand through his thinning hair as he lifted his cap.

"You missed your appointment this morning," she said in frustration.

"I had an appointment today?" he asked, feigning forgetfulness. He didn't like visiting his cardiologist.

"Dad! Yes, you did."

"I guess I did miss it, Cathy," he grinned sheepishly.

"Oh Dad. Can you go this afternoon if they have an opening?"

"Give me a minute to think what I have to do this afternoon." The man turned to wave at the little girl who was walking away to board the ferry. He knew that he didn't have anything planned that afternoon.

"I guess my calendar is clear. I can go this afternoon."

"I know what you're up to Mr. Zeke Layne."

"What?" he asked innocently.

"You're going to conveniently forget that you have the appointment if I reset it."

"Would I do that?"

"Yes, you would. You're lucky I have the day off. I'm driving you there," she said indignantly. She handed him a brown paper bag with his lunch. "I'll give the office a call," she said.

She then turned and walked back to their mobile home.

"Just as fiery and lovely as Leona," Layne mused. He'd let Cathy drive him. Every year as he aged, he didn't like driving as much. Maybe it was because of the times that he would get lost and have to pull off the road. He'd either walk to a nearby house or call his good friend and local sign painter, Jerry Davenport to ask for directions. He had restricted his driving to the Catawba Peninsula and to Port Clinton, but that was becoming more of a challenge to him.

CHAPTER 2

Heading to the Doctor
Catawba Peninsula, Ohio

As they drove down West Catawba Road, Cathy admonished her father. "Dad, you really do need to keep these doctor appointments."

"I forgot," he answered weakly.

"Do you forget your Friday night beer party at the dock?"

"No."

"Do you forget your euchre party at the Catawba Inn?"

"No," he answered meekly.

"I didn't think so. We write everything on the calendar in the kitchen so none of us forget where we have to be. Your events are on there, too."

"My Friday night beer party isn't."

"Dad. Like you would ever forget that! We all know where you'll be on Friday night. In fact, I think the entire peninsula knows where you are on Friday night," she said in a half-serious tone.

The car continued onto East Sand Road, which hung the beautiful cliffs overlooking Lake Erie and the small beach fifty feet below.

In the distance, the Jet Express was flying on the wave tops as it carried a load of passengers from downtown Port Clinton to Put-in-Bay. On the horizon, a white plume of smoke escaped from the tall cooling tower of the Davis Besse nuclear power plant. It looked like a huge smoking cigar.

"I've always loved this part of the ride to Port Clinton. It's so scenic," Layne commented with a smile as he took in the view.

"Don't try changing the subject on me, Dad. I'm wise to your tricks."

Layne wrinkled his brow and frowned at her remark. Caught again.

"That calendar is there for an emergency if any one of us had to find the other."

"I thought that's why you got me a cell phone," he countered.

"That helps too. But we know where each of us is. You know when I work..."

"Most every night," he interrupted.

"And when I have off. You know when Michelle is at work."

"But you know my routine. I'm a creature of habit."

"You are for the most part. Every day we know you go to the ferry dock and spend most of your day there."

"Except for when it storms."

"I know. You come home."

"And you know I go see the horse on Mondays, Wednesdays and Fridays. She's got to have her carrots from me." He was referring to Michelle's horse, Irish Gin, who was stabled on South Bass Island.

"I know. But we don't know when you go over to Jerry's or disappear to wherever," she said firmly.

"I didn't know I was under close supervision, warden."

"You should be." She was worried about him. Layne was becoming disoriented more often and frequently lost. It seemed like it was happening two to three times a week now.

The car turned right onto East Perry Street. Within ten minutes, they parked and entered the lobby of the hospital. They next walked into the office of cardiologist Dr. John Schaffner and checked in with the receptionist before taking a seat.

"Mr. Layne?" a voice called from behind them.

Layne stood and pulled his wallet out. He opened it and showed the nurse the driver's license photo. "I guess that's me," he teased as he folded the wallet and replaced it in his back pocket.

"Zeke, you do this every time you come in here," she commented.

"It's a good thing I do, Mary Alice. You wouldn't want to take the wrong patient back, would you?"

"You know my dad," Cathy chipped in as she smiled.

"Like I could forget how he teased us when we had slumber parties at your place as kids?" Mary Alice quipped. "I remember that one time when he came into the living room with a sheet over his head and made spooky noises," she smiled.

"Scared you all, didn't I?" Layne beamed. He walked slowly, but rather steady for a man of his years and condition.

"You remember that?" Mary Alice asked.

As Layne nodded, Cathy added, "Dad doesn't seem to forget pranks that he's pulled on people."

They all chuckled.

"Pull any good ones lately, Zeke?"

"Yeah. This morning a kid left his helium balloon behind. I saw a bunch of people running down the hill to catch the ferry before they raised the ramp. Just before they got to me, I took a lung full of helium and in my best voice, told them to hurry and follow the yellow brick road. You should have seen the looks on their faces."

As they laughed, he added, "Then I took the balloon and tied it to the back of my suspenders. When some more people showed up, I told them that I thought I was being followed and walked away from them."

"You will never change," Mary Alice said. She grinned a little, too, as she led them down the hall to the examination room.

"I hope not," Layne said although he didn't like the reality of his advancing Alzheimer's.

"Let me take your temperature," Mary Alice said. She produced a thermometer and inserted it into Layne's mouth. She then reached for his wrist. "I'm going to take your pulse."

"This tastes funny. You sure you didn't just give me a rectal thermometer?" Layne joked.

The nurse shook her head from side to side. "You are just incorrigible." She reached for the thermometer and looked at it. "Temp is normal." She entered that information into his medical records. "Now let's take your blood pressure."

The nurse placed the cuff around his arm and began inflating it. "Are you taking all of your meds, Zeke?"

"Most of the time."

"Zeke, you need to take them as prescribed. No skipping. And no ifs or buts," she said sternly.

"We're going to talk about butts?"

"Only if you want me to jab a sharp needle in yours," she cracked.

Subdued, Layne shook his head negatively and took off his glasses. He pulled a handkerchief from his pocket, cleaned them and replaced them on his head.

"Sounds like there's a lot of fun going on in here," a tall man with graying hair said while walking into the room. He was wearing a white lab coat and had a stethoscope hung around his neck. It was Dr. Schaffner.

"Join the party Doctor," Layne suggested.

"Where's your cowboy hat?" Layne added, knowing how much Schaffner enjoyed wearing one.

As the nurse began to walk out of the room, she leaned toward the doctor. "Blood pressure is high."

Schaffner nodded as he took a seat on the wheeled stool. "How have you been feeling, Zeke?"

"Just my ornery old self."

Schaffner looked at Cathy who nodded.

"Been taking your meds, Zeke?" he asked while reading Layne's medical records.

"When I remember, I do."

"Or he doesn't drop them on the floor and leave them for me to pick up. Then I have to track him down to make sure he takes what he's supposed to take," Cathy offered.

"I don't need all of them pills anyway," Layne retorted.

Schaffner turned back to Layne. "Yes, you do. Otherwise, I wouldn't prescribe them. I want to take your blood pressure again." Schaffner began to wrap the cuff around Layne's arm, then stopped. "No, I think I want a bigger cuff."

"Cup size? DD works just fine for me," Layne quipped.

"Your sense of humor never changes, does it, Zeke?"

Schaffner wrapped a bigger cuff around Layne's bicep and squeezed the bulb to inflate it. He listened through his stethoscope as the cuff deflated. As he wrote down the blood pressure, he asked Cathy. "Is he like this at home? Does he ever slow down with his kidding?"

"He's like this any time he has an audience."

Schaffner turned to Layne. "Zeke, your pressure is 180 over 100. That is not good. When you were here thirty days ago, I recommended heart surgery and you said no."

"And if that's what you're going to say again, I'm going to say no again," Layne countered quickly.

"This is serious, Zeke."

Any mirth that had been evident in Layne disappeared as he squinted his eyes and said, "Doc, I've had a good life and I've got this Alzheimer's stuff creeping up on me. I know it. That's reality. I don't want to put my family through it. I'm not going to be a burden on anyone. Never have been. Never will be. If my way out is through heart failure, then so be it."

"And what if your heart complication doesn't result in death. What if you have a stroke and become disabled?"

Layne jumped right in. "Then pull the plug on me and put me out of my misery. I want to be clear to both of you." He turned to Cathy. "You understand me, Honey?"

"I do, Dad," she said as tears filled her eyes. That was not a day that she looked forward to.

"I'm making a note here in the medical records that we had this discussion again."

"You go right ahead and make whatever notes you want, Doc. My will is in order and I have my Do Not Resuscitate completed too. I'm a planner."

"I know you are Zeke and we have a copy of your DNR in our files." The doctor looked directly at Layne. "Do you still have the nitroglycerine pills I earlier prescribed?"

Layne patted his pants pocket. "Right here."

"Have you had to take any since I last saw you?"

"Once."

"What happened?"

Cathy butted in. "I can answer that. He got upset with me when I took his car keys away from him. It was storming real bad and he wanted to drive over to Jerry Davenport's place."

"Zeke, tell me why you took the nitro."

"I felt like my face was getting flushed."

"Probably your blood pressure was up," Schaffner suggested.

"And I felt a tightness in my chest. I know the sign and popped one real quick like," Layne explained.

"You keep them handy. Do you have any questions for me?" the doctor asked.

"Yes."

"What?"

"Can I go now?"

Schaffner nodded his head. "Yes. I'll send in Mary Alice. It was good seeing both of you," he said as he stood and shook hands with Layne.

"Yeah. Yeah." Layne was not happy with the exchange. If they had taken his blood pressure at that moment, they would have seen that it was higher.

"I'm still waiting for an invite to join your Lounge Lizard band. You need a blues harp player?"

"I've told you before that anytime we perform, and you attend that you can sit in for a song," Schaffner offered. "Do you remember?"

Layne wrinkled his brow as he thought. "Well, I guess you did."

"Take us up on it, Zeke. You are more than welcome. And be sure to take your pills. All of them," Schaffner cautioned.

Layne grumbled under his breath as Schaffner left the room.

Minutes later, Mary Alice entered to escort them to the lobby. When they reached it, Layne turned to her.

"Do I get a hug?"

"You still pulling that schtick on women?" she laughed.

"Only the pretty ones," Layne cracked as the two embraced.

"You know how my dad is with pretty women," Cathy smiled.

"That is one constant in his life," Mary Alice agreed, hugging him.

Finished with the hug, Layne said, "Now let's go home."

"There's one more stop, Dad."

"What?"

"I checked with Doctor Egan before we left the house and he can see you while we are here."

"I don't like him," Layne grumbled. "I'm going outside."

"Oh, come on, Dad. It will just be a quick visit."

"I don't need any more bad news today," Layne shot back angrily. He started walking toward the exit door.

"He might want to talk about fishing."

Layne paused for a moment and thought about her comment. "No way. I've had my quota of doctors today."

"I'm going to see him."

"You can see whoever you want. I'm going outside to wait for you," he replied firmly.

She recognized his tone and knew that there was no way that she would get him to change his mind. "Okay, but don't wander off."

"I won't. I'll just sit over there on one of the benches."

Cathy walked down the white-tiled hallway and entered Dr. D'Arcy Egan's office. As she approached the desk to register, Dr. Egan opened the door to allow a patient to leave.

"Hello Cathy. Perfect timing," he said in motioning her to walk through. "Where's your dad?"

"Outside. He didn't want to see two doctors today. He actually snapped at me."

"That doesn't sound like him. He's pretty easy going." Egan turned to the receptionist and explained, "She's here on behalf of Zeke Layne. Could you go ahead and sign him in."

He turned back to Cathy and spoke, "Follow me."

D'Arcy Egan had gone to high school with Cathy and knew the family well. He was the area's top neurologist and was also known for his fishing skills. Over the years, he and Layne together had gone on several fishing adventures.

As they entered his office, he pointed to one of the chairs for Cathy and he sat in the other.

"How's your dad doing?"

"He's getting more forgetful. He's started having problems balancing his checkbook. He was one who could make a quick decision and now he struggles with making them. He can't remember where he puts things. I don't know how much of this is just due to old age or Alzheimer's."

Egan nodded his head as he listened.

"And he's upset that many of his old friends are dying."

"That happens when you start getting up there in age."

Cathy cracked a smile before she continued. "He started buying sympathy cards in bulk, but there was one problem."

"What was that?"

"He bought birthday cards instead and has been sending them out by mistake to the grieving family. I really do need to supervise him more closely."

"Oh no! It sounds like his cognitive thinking is regressing. He really needs to be in here for some more tests," Egan urged.

Cathy sighed before commenting. "I think he really struggles with coming here. He's always liked you, but I think he's afraid of what you're going to tell him."

"It sounds like he's transitioning into the next stage. You might recall that we diagnosed him as being in moderate decline because of his simple arithmetic problems and short-term memory loss. Have you asked him what he's had for breakfast lately?"

"I do that a couple of times a week and he can't remember. And that's weird because he has the same breakfast every day. Corn flakes or toast."

Egan shook his head from side to side. "I'm concerned. Can he remember his phone number?"

"Yes. I ask him once a week. So far, he has remembered it, but he also thinks I'm goofy for asking."

"What about getting dressed. Have you noticed any difficulty? Do his outfits go together?"

"Yes, although one day he came out fully dressed, but he had Michelle's panties on his head like a hat," she chuckled softly as she recalled the incident.

A look of concern crossed Egan's face. "That worries me. His mental acuity is not what it should be."

"I think he knew what he was doing because he asked why her panties were in his underwear drawer. I must have got them mixed up with his when I put away the laundry."

Egan snickered. "He still has his famous sense of humor."

"That he does. He never seems to forget the pranks he pulls on people. Sometimes, I think he says that he forgets things because he doesn't want to do them. Like this morning, he forgot about his appointment with Dr. Schaffner."

"That does make it hard to evaluate. I have one patient tell me that she will tell her family members that she can't answer their question, because she can't remember. She told me that she does remember, but she doesn't want to answer their questions."

"That's funny," Cathy chuckled. A more serious look crossed her face. "There's one more thing."

"What's that?"

"Dad went out on the deck. He likes to fish from it in the early evening at times. I asked him if he was catching any fish and he said they weren't biting. He was pretty frustrated."

"They don't always bite," Egan said. "I know that all too well from a lot of personal experience."

"I know that, but there's a reason. I've started going out on the deck to watch him get set up for fishing. I see him attach the bobber and sinker, but he forgets to attach the hook. He just drops the line in without a hook."

"Has this happened often?"

"It's happened on four occasions. I work most nights so I'm not there to watch. I've asked Michelle to watch when she's home and she saw it happen twice."

"That's a concern, though I admit I've had my own share of fishing miscues over the years. We need to keep an eye on Zeke. You never know how it will progress. It could be over a number of years or overnight. You just don't know for sure."

"I understand. I'll keep a close eye on him," she assured the doctor. He stood, signaling the end of their appointment.

"Let me give you these cards."

"What are these?"

"They're 'Pardon My Companion' cards for when Zeke misbehaves in a public setting. You just hand one to the person he may have possibly offended and it explains that he has Alzheimer's."

"What a great idea!" she said in taking the cards. "I can make good use of these."

"Tell Zeke I said hello," Egan offered. He then opened the door and she departed. "Call if you need anything."

"I'll be sure to tell him."

As she exited the building, she spotted Layne. He was talking to Jerry Davenport, the local sign maker, who just finished installing a new sign for the hospital.

"Hi Jerry," she called. Cathy approached the gray-haired, fifty-year-old man. He also was a local entertainer with his guitar and harmonica. He preferred that one referred to it as a blues harp. Davenport and Layne would get together in the evenings at Davenport's Catawba chalet on the edge of Barnum Cove to play the blues harp together. If she couldn't find Layne, Davenport was always her first call.

Davenport was a lifelong Catawba resident and attended Ohio State University where he bought his first blues harp at the big Lazarus department store in downtown Columbus. He started his musical career by writing poetry and soon progressed to lyrics for his music. He accidentally got into the sign business when his wife said no to his aspiring career as a musician.

Davenport was very talented and creative. He was very likeable and was more of an introvert with some extrovert tendencies.

"Hello Cathy," Davenport responded in his warm, gravelly voice.

"Is my dad keeping you from your work?"

"Work? Jerry doesn't work. He's on break most of the day. I don't know how he gets anything done," Layne interjected.

Davenport smiled. "I was just finishing up. He's never a

bother, Cathy."

"You two are always up to no good when you get together."

"That's the best way to be, isn't it Zeke?" Davenport asked.

"The only way!"

Holding out several of the "Pardon My Companion" cards that Egan had recently given her, Cathy offered, "Take a few of these Jerry. You might need to use them if you and Dad go anywhere."

"What have we here?" Davenport asked in reading the card quickly.

"What is it?" Layne asked. He tried to read the card.

"Just a 'Get out of Jail Free' card to use around you when you say something inappropriate to people," Davenport explained.

"You better order several dozen of them cards then," Layne countered.

"Exactly what I was thinking, Zeke," Davenport agreed. "I should have my wife order some for her to use with me," he chuckled.

"Come on, Dad. We need to let Jerry get back to his work and I need to get you home."

"See you later, Jerry," Layne said. They walked away and entered the car. "You working tonight?"

"No. I have tonight off, Dad. I'm going to make your favorite dinner. It will be just for the two of us because Michelle is working tonight."

"Meatloaf?"

"Yes."

"Like your mother made?"

"Yes. I always use her recipe and you ask me every time."

"I know I do. I just want to be sure that you don't make it

any other way. It reminds me of her when I eat it," he said wistfully as they headed for home. Layne was quiet for the entire ride as he reflected on how much he missed the love of his life.

His silence was not lost on Cathy. She noticed it was happening more often that he was having more melancholy moods. It concerned her even though he'd try to hide it when he was out of the trailer.

When she pulled into their drive, she stopped the car and reached over to take Layne's hand.

"Dad?"

"What?" he asked. He looked from her hand holding his up to her face.

"Are you okay?"

"I am," he assured her.

"You were pretty quiet on the ride home."

"I was thinking."

"About?"

"Your mother."

"You miss her, don't you?"

"I do. She was the love of my life."

Layne then allowed his gaze to drift toward the lake where the waves were breaking against the rocks. He then turned back toward Cathy and offered, "I'll be fine. Now, you get yourself in that kitchen and fix me that meatloaf."

She gave him a quick smile and the two exited the car. As Cathy entered the trailer, Sheba appeared from around the corner with her tail wagging a bit wildly and tried to jump on Layne.

"Missed me, didn't you?" Layne smiled as he rubbed her head.

Sheba barked in response as he knelt down beside her.

"That's my girl. I love you, too."

Sheba broke away and trotted behind the house. When she returned, she had the ball in her mouth.

"Okay. Okay," Layne smiled as he took the ball from her. They walked around the mobile home and he threw the ball in the water. The two played fetch and retrieve for the next twenty minutes. Layne then went into the house and Sheba sought out the late afternoon sun on the deck to dry her coat.

Later that evening, Layne was sitting on the deck. He absent-mindedly rubbed Sheba while he watched the twilight turn into night. His mind was clouded with gray as his mood sank. He had no energy or motivation.

His face grimaced and contorted into a painful expression. It was at moments like these that he felt alone and drowning in his emotions. The enduring grief from losing his first wife would well up. He missed Leona dearly. His daughter and granddaughter's presence helped as did their love, but he still felt alone. Tears trickled down his face as waves of remorse swept over Layne.

His remorse, his fear, was that he now realized he was sometimes unable to recall the years together with Leona. Perhaps it was simply forgetting her name when he thought of her. Upon another occasion, Layne might not remember the couple had been married, or for how long. Sometimes, but rarely, he believed she might still be alive, but was missing for some unknown reason and that explained her prolonged absence.

"Dad, can I join you?"

Quickly wiping the tears away with the back of his hand, Layne tried to bury those emotions as he replied, "Sure. Grab a seat." He removed his glasses. He pulled a handkerchief from his pocket, cleaned them and replaced them on his head.

"What are you doing out here?"

"Watching the night cover the lake like a blanket," he said.

She smiled. He would often use that line. She grabbed a chair and set it next to him. "Sure is a pretty evening."

"Every evening here is, especially when you don't have to work and can join me."

"Charmer!" she teased. "I just love it here. It's so peaceful after all of the day traffic is gone."

"It's going to be a good night for stargazing," Layne observed. The twinkling stars appeared in the distant sky.

"That's something special you do with Michelle — identifying stars together."

"When she's home. If she's not working, she's running with her friends."

"She still makes time for you," Cathy reminded him.

"I know. You both do."

"No cards tonight?"

"Nope. The guys are busy."

Several nights a week, a bunch of Layne's friends would gather at the Catawba Inn for burgers and beer before playing euchre for a few hours. It was a long tradition of theirs. Other nights, Layne would be at Jerry Davenport's house to play the blues harp together.

"Tonight, I have you all to myself," Cathy said cheerfully.

"Not much to have."

"Dad, don't say that. You're just having a bad day. You're out of sorts."

"I am out of sorts. Been thinking about your mom and life."

"I miss her."

"I do, too," he agreed.

"You used to sit out here with her."

"I did. It was our quiet time together. She'd have a glass of wine and I'd have my beer. Together, we'd sort out the day's troubles and put them behind us."

"Nothing like having someone like her at your side."

"She was one of a kind, but so are you. I see a lot of her in you. You're kind and tenderhearted like she was."

"Thanks Dad. I try to be like her in a lot of ways."

"You're doing a good job. Keep it up," he said as he turned and looked at her.

"That I will. I promise. Cross my heart and hope to die," she said as she crossed her heart. It was something that her mother would do and Layne had picked it up as well as Michelle.

"Just like your mother."

"I take that as a compliment."

"And you should." He paused before continuing. "We'd always look for the North Star. We'd agreed that if anything ever happened to either of us, that star would serve as a reminder of our love for each other. Any time we saw it, it was to remind us," he said as he looked up and spotted it.

"Just like now," Cathy concurred while looking up at it. She stood and walked over to Layne. Placing her arms around him, she gave him a kiss on the cheek. "I love you, Dad."

He patted her arm. "I know you do. I love you too, sweetie."

They stayed in that position for another couple of minutes before she spoke again. "I'm going to head in." She gave him another kiss on the cheek. "I love you, Dad."

Layne smiled as she walked away. He then reached into his pocket and pulled out his harmonica. He brought it to his lips and began playing Garth Brooks' song *If Tomorrow Never Comes*. The soulful tune waffled out over the waves and the nearby ferry dock.

After a couple of minutes, he slipped the harmonica back into his pocket and went inside for the night.

CHAPTER 3

Miller Ferry Catawba Dock
The Next Day

Layne was enjoying the day. He'd again been entertaining the waiting passengers with his harmonica playing and stories while children gathered around to pet Sheba, who was sitting at his feet.

Layne suddenly stopped playing his harmonica and looked out the window into the blue sky. Pointing skyward with his finger, he loudly declared, "Look, there's a dead seagull."

As people turned to look, Layne let out a round of guffaws as people fell for his prank. A little boy sidled up to him and said, "I didn't see one."

Layne had a fun-loving smile on his face. "Sonny, that's the joke. Dead seagulls don't fly."

A smile crossed the boy's face as he understood the explanation. "I get it. That's funny, mister."

"Oh, you haven't seen anything." Layne pointed to a silver dollar on the floor. "Think you can pick up that coin over there?"

"I can!"

"Go and do it, then."

The boy ran across the waiting area and bent over to pick

it up. He tried and tried, but couldn't budge it. He returned to Layne's side. "I couldn't pick it up."

"No one can. I super glued it to the floor," Layne chortled as a frown crossed the boy's face. "But you can watch other people try to pick it up."

The frown disappeared and was replaced by a conspiratorial grin as they watched two other children trying to pick up the coin.

After ten minutes, Layne reached into a small cooler he had next to him. "Would you like a cold water?"

The boy looked at his mother, who was standing nearby. "Is it okay, Mom?"

"As long as it hasn't been opened," she replied. She also looked to Layne for affirmation.

"Lady, I can guarantee this water hasn't been opened," Layne said with a sly look. He handed the bottle to the boy.

The boy tried, but couldn't open it.

"I can't get it open," he moaned as he tried again.

"Keep trying."

"I can't get it," the boy said in frustration. He handed the bottle back to Layne.

The old man began laughing. "That's because, my boy, the cap is glued on."

The boy frowned at being tricked, then a smile crossed his face. "Can you give it to my sister?"

The mother intervened. "I don't think so," she said as she gave Layne a wink.

The boy frowned again.

"I've got another trick we can pull, and you can help me."

The boy's expression changed immediately. "What are we going to do?" He now was eager to pull a prank on someone.

Layne reached into his bag and pulled out a small walkie-talkie radio. He handed it to the boy while instructing him to shout aloud "get me out of here."

"Why?" the boy curiously asked, not quite understanding the intended trickery.

"Because, I hid another walkie-talkie in that trash can over there."

The boy looked to where Layne pointed and spied the trash can. He also saw two passengers approaching it. Raising the walkie-talkie to his mouth, he shouted, "Get me out of here!"

For the next five minutes, the boy pranked passengers and giggled at their reactions while Layne played his harmonica.

When it was time to board the ferry, the boy reluctantly returned the walkie-talkie to Layne. "Thank you."

"You're welcome, Sonny."

As the boy walked over to his family, a woman standing nearby asked, "Have you ever been on the ferry in the lake during a lightning storm?"

"I have and more than once. One time, lightning struck the masthead light. There was a big flash and that milk jug-sized light broke into 8,000 pieces. It took two days before that ozone taste left my mouth."

"Oh my," she said. "What about the fog?"

"That was my downfall," Layne answered.

"How's that?"

"It was so thick out there that I made a wrong turn and I was headed to go over Niagara Falls," he teased her. "That was the day I became retired."

"Oh no!" the woman said with a horrified look.

"Grandpa," a voice called over Layne's shoulder.

Recognizing it right away, Layne responded, "Did you bring

me my carrots?" He turned in his seat and saw his granddaughter approaching. In her hand, she carried three carrots.

"Yes. You forgot them on the kitchen counter," Michelle said as she handed them to Layne.

"When do you have to go to work?"

"Not for an hour and a half."

"Want to come with me? We can still catch the ferry."

"No."

"Oh, come on. Keep me company."

She took a deep breath and sighed. "Oh, all right. If it makes you happy." She took his outstretched hand and they headed for the ferry. "I guess it's a nice day for a ferry ride."

"Every day is a good day for a ferry ride," Layne said. "Come on Sheba. We're going for a ferry ride."

Sheba alertly arose to her feet and wagged her tail at the thought of riding the ferry.

"Couple more passengers, Matt," Layne shouted. The last passengers rapidly approached the ferry ramp.

Parker turned and called to the deck crew, who were getting ready to raise the ramp. "Hold up there. Got three more."

The three scurried aboard.

As the ramp closed behind them, they walked past the parked vehicles and around several passengers who were jockeying for position to stand in the bow area. Layne stopped midship and said, "Let's stand here. We're in for a treat," he said. He looked at the passengers in the bow with a sense of anticipation.

"First timers?" Michelle asked, already knowing the answer from prior ferry rides.

"Yep," Layne smiled. "It's wet tee shirt contest time," he chuckled. He had heard that the South Passage had been stirring up that afternoon and knew that sizeable waves would be breaking over the bow.

The blast of the ferry's horn and the increased rumble of her diesel engines signaled that she was reversing out of the dock. Once she cleared the dock, she pointed her bow for South Bass Island and started her run. Ten minutes later and much to the delight of Layne and Michelle, several waves broke over the bow, drenching the shrieking passengers.

The two were giggling as they watched the passengers scurry midship.

"That reminds me of a story," Layne said as he removed his glasses. He pulled a handkerchief from his pocket, cleaned his glasses and replaced them on his head.

"Is it another long one?" Michelle well knew her grandfather's habit of telling long stories as well as repeating stories that he had already told her.

"It's not long to me," he said before continuing with a story about his days working on the ferry. It was one he repeated often to her – and to her dismay.

After another ten minutes passed, the ferry approached South Bass Island's Lime Kiln dock. As she neared the dock, her horn blasted to announce her arrival and she swung around to her berth as the loudspeaker explained that the vehicles would first disembark before the passengers. The stern ramp lowered and the deckhands guided the vehicles off the ferry and toward the drive up the hill to Langram Road.

The passengers then exited the ferry for the challenging walk up the steep hill to the waiting lines of taxis and buses for a ride to downtown Put-in-Bay. Some passengers opted for the nearby golf cart rentals.

Layne and Michelle walked down the ferry ramp and turned right. They went past the lines of waiting cars for the return trip to the Catawba dock and headed for the freight barns.

Layne looked fondly at Barn 1, which was built in the early 1900's. It was originally a twine shanty where fishing nets were repaired. He sometimes recalled the stories from the old-timers who long ago had spent many hours working there.

When he, along with Michelle and Sheba, rounded the back of Barn 4, they saw the corral with two ponies. A small boy was riding a paint. It was Liam Market, the five-year-old son of Billy and Allie Market.

"Hi Liam. You look comfortable in that saddle," Layne called.

"I am, Mr. Layne," Liam said. The young lad trotted the horse over to the fence. "I'm going to teach him tricks. Hi Michelle."

"Hi Liam. Every time I see you, you look older."

"I am. I get older every day."

"Just like me," another voice called.

Layne and Michelle turned and saw Billy walking toward them.

"Aren't we all?" Layne quipped.

"Everyone but the pretty Michelle," Billy teased.

"Billy, you need to get your eyes checked," Michelle countered.

Billy laughed and asked her, "You going to ride Irish Gin today?"

"I don't think so."

She looked at the golden palomino that was approaching them and remained fearful. A year ago, she had taken a bad tumble when she was riding along Langram Road. Two drunks in a golf cart had spooked the horse and drove away. Irish Gin reared and threw her before bolting all of the way back to the corral.

She didn't break any bones, but was badly bruised as was her comfort level around horses. After laying on the side of the road, she rose to her feet. She had an enormous headache as she walked slowly back to the corral. She let Irish Gin in the corral and caught the next ferry back to Catawba and home. She never rode again.

"One of these days, my little princess will ride again," Layne said in an encouraging tone.

"Not any day soon," she replied. Michelle looked at the horse rather blankly.

It was as if Irish Gin knew that the humans were talking about her. She neighed and bobbed her head as she saw the carrots in Layne's hand.

"Oh, okay, my hungry lass. Have one," Layne offered. He held out one of the carrots which Irish Gin chomped on. As he fed her, he said, "Billy, I do appreciate you guys taking care of her."

"That's no problem. Lucky for you that Liam has a horse here and it all worked out for you to keep yours here. Had an extra stall that no one was using."

"Let me show you and Liam a trick I've been working on with Irish Gin," Layne said, in turning to the horse. He raised his hands and commanded, "Up!"

Irish Gin raised her front legs and stood on her rear legs. At the same time, she let loose with a loud whinny and Sheba barked her approval.

"Impressive," Billy said. The horse lowered her front legs and her head nuzzled Layne as she looked for another carrot.

"Yep. I'm thinking I'm going to move up and start training lions next," Layne said with a twinkle in his eye.

"Really? You're going to bring a lion over here?" Liam exclaimed excitedly.

"He's just kidding Liam," Billy responded.

"You never know," Layne cracked as he ran his hands through the horse's mane.

"It's getting late and Allie is grilling steak for dinner. We better put your horse away, son."

"Okay," Liam said reluctantly. The two headed for the barn entrance.

They exchanged farewells and Layne turned to Michelle. "Want to surprise me and take a ride?"

Michelle looked at her horse. "I'm just not ready, Grandpa."

"Okay. I understand, but one day I just know you'll be riding her again. Cross my heart and hope to die," he said in crossing his heart.

Michelle uncomfortably smiled at her grandfather, unsure that she could fulfill his wish.

He turned back to the horse, "Up!"

The horse repeated the trick and looked for a carrot which Layne promptly gave her.

"Grandpa, I need to get back. It's almost time for me to go to work."

"Sure. Sure," Layne said as he fed the horse the last carrot. "We'll see you another day Irish Gin."

The horse whinnied as the two with Sheba walked away to the dock for the return ride to Catawba.

After they reached the mainland, Layne saw Matt Parker and stayed to talk with him before heading home. Michelle walked quickly to the trailer. When she entered, she saw her mother in the kitchen.

"Mom," she moaned.

"What, Honey?"

"It's Grandpa."

"What did he do now?"

"He talks so much. It's like watching a bad movie."

"What do you mean, Honey?"

"You want to hit fast forward and get to the end. He went on and on to repeat some stupid stories on the ride over to feed Irish Gin. His stories take forever!" she groaned.

Cathy glanced at her watch to be sure that she wouldn't be late for work.

"All grandparents are like that. They love to reminisce about the old days."

"Oh, but he just rambles."

"You need to be tolerant. Sometimes it's hard for him to focus. It's his Alzheimer's."

"Can you explain that to me?"

"Simply put, it's like this electric cord to the radio. If the current is interrupted, the music is interrupted. His brain waves get interrupted and cause gaps in his thinking and memory. It's like his brain takes a detour at times."

"I always knew he had a short circuit somewhere," Michelle sighed.

"It's like your hard drive on your computer is missing data or when a record skips. There's a gap."

"I get it. It's like his brain crashes," Michelle said as she understood. "Sometimes he seems so normal and thinking right. Other times, he's so forgetful."

"I know, and Honey, it's going to get worse." Cathy glanced at her watch again. "I have to run, or I will be late."

Michelle looked at the kitchen clock. "I didn't realize it was that late. I've got to get to the Dairy Dock."

The two women left the trailer. Cathy walked across the Miller Ferry parking lot to the Catawba Inn on North Crogan Street and Michelle walked along Water Street that fronted the lake to her job at the ice cream stand. Shortly after they left, Layne returned to the trailer.

An hour later Matt Parker knocked on the door. "Zeke, ready to go play some cards?"

"Be right there," Layne said. He opened the door. "What are you wearing, Matt?"

"You like?"

"I think it's real funny."

The light blue tee shirt read "Graduate – The Bud Ohlemacher School of Charm."

"Does Bud know you have that?" Layne asked. He thought about the cantankerous and crusty ferry worker, who was anything but charming.

"Not yet," Parker smiled. They walked with Sheba to the Catawba Inn, the aqua blue-painted, two-story inn on the other side of the ferry parking lot. The side of the building had two words painted in bright blue – Food and Beer.

"Did you lock the front door?" Parker asked as he looked back at Layne's home.

"No. There's nothing to steal. If robbers broke into my trailer and began searching for money, I'd help them to see if we'd find any. Then we could split it," Layne chortled.

Parker shook his head as he grinned at his friend. They headed for the rear deck where Jerry Davenport and Kenny Kartheiser were sitting.

"Ready for some euchre?" Layne greeted the men who were waiting patiently as they nursed their drinks.

"You bet," Kartheiser said. The men exchanged greetings and Sheba sat on the deck next to Layne.

An attractive server appeared. She was slender with dark brown hair and even darker brown eyes. Her name was Kylah Meagan.

"Hi Matt. Hi Zeke," she greeted her regulars.

"Do I get my hug?" Layne teased as he leaned back in his chair.

"Don't you always, you scoundrel?"

"That's some schtick you got there, Zeke," Davenport joked as Kylah wrapped her arms around Layne.

"But it works," Layne grinned with a twinkle in his eyes.

"Yeah, and he gets away with it because, at his age, every woman thinks he's harmless," Parker added. "And he calls it his happytizer!"

"Don't go and upset my apple cart, Matt. You let them think that," Layne said as Kylah ended the hug and got down to business.

"The usual?" she asked Parker and Layne.

"Yes," Parker replied.

"Great googly moogly! I always get the same," Layne chimed in. "And don't forget that layer of peanut butter on my burger."

"Zeke, have I ever forgot to add it?" she asked with a look of exasperation.

"No, but you just never know when you might get forget-ful."

"I'm not the forgetful one," she shot back. She knew all about Layne's progressing Alzheimer's. "Who is the only one in this group who always forgets his wallet?"

Davenport jumped right in. "That's not being forgetful,

Kylah. That's his strategy."

They all roared as she walked away.

Calling after Kylah, Layne added, "Tell Cathy I'm here. She's always fretting about me."

"I will," she said as she entered the building.

"You need one of them chains that attach your wallet to your pants so you don't forget it," Kartheiser suggested. They all knew that Cathy ended up paying for his meals and drinks.

"I need Cathy to drive me over to see Lonnie Morris. It's been a while," Layne said. Being with his friends reminded him of his former co-worker.

"He's over at that nursing home in Sandusky, isn't he?" Parker asked as he shuffled the cards.

"Yeah."

"How's he doing?" Kartheiser asked.

"Not so good the last time I saw him. His memory is really going." Layne chuckled in recalling the visit two months ago. "When I walked in his room, he had a suppository sticking out of his ear. I can't remember which ear it was, but it was the funniest thing."

"Did you tell him?" Davenport asked.

"I did."

"What did he do?"

"He pulled it out and looked at it. Then he said that he thought he knew where his missing hearing aid was."

The men laughed even though it was the third time Layne had told that story.

"That's funny," Kartheiser said to his friend.

Layne turned around to look at a table behind them. There were two men and four women sitting around it and they were laughing. Layne turned back around and spoke. "Did you hear what they thought was so funny?"

"No," Davenport replied as the other two shook their heads negatively.

"The blonde was trying to figure out why she has only three sisters and her brother has four sisters. That's what got them laughing."

The other three men laughed at the comment.

Layne smiled and looked toward the building. "I gotta go."

"Where?" Davenport asked.

"The jim."

Davenport smiled. "You're the only guy I know who says that he's going to the jim rather than the john because it sounds better."

"No, I really do," Layne said with an agitated look on his face.

"Well, go then," Davenport said.

Layne now had a confused look on his face, one that his friends had seen before. "I can't."

"Why? Did you wet your pants?" Parker jested.

There was no joking in the tone that Layne used. His frustration erupted. "I can't remember where it is!" he stormed.

"Easy. Easy," Davenport said in his typical calm fashion. "I'll walk you over," he said as the two men stood.

"Thank you," Layne said appreciatively. "I just can't remember."

"Just so you know that all I'm doing is walking you over there. I'm not coming in with you," Davenport explained as they walked toward the building.

"I don't need help inside. I just don't know where it is."

Davenport watched as Layne walked into the men's room, then returned to the table.

"Not good," Parker said.

"I know," Davenport agreed. "How has he been on the dock."

"Pretty good. We see him doing some stuff that's weird. But not too bad."

"Not like a couple of weeks ago when he got his haircut, and someone stole his truck," Kartheiser added.

"Right," Davenport agreed.

"I didn't hear about that one. What happened?" Parker asked.

"He drove over to that little strip mall to get a haircut. When he walked out, he couldn't find his truck. He went back inside and called the police. The police came out and took the report. When he described the truck, the officer pointed to one parked a few spots down from the barber shop and asked if that was it. Zeke got all upset and said it was his. He claimed that he didn't park it there and that someone moved it even though he had the keys in his pocket."

"Oh no," Parker moaned.

"I brought it up to Zeke a couple of times and he still claims that someone moved it while he was getting a haircut," Kartheiser added.

"I think he's slipping," Davenport observed.

"You guys talking about me?" Layne asked. He returned to the table just as Kylah appeared with the food. "Hey, where's my hug? I didn't get a hug."

"We were just wondering where our food was," Kartheiser commented.

"Perfect timing, boys," Kylah said. She then served the men their orders. "And Zeke, you already got a hug from me, dear." She left, then returned in a few minutes. "I brought a bowl of water for Sheba, too".

Kylah placed the water bowl on the deck. Sheba immediately approached it and began lapping it up.

"Sheba says thank you," Layne offered. He broke off a piece of his burger and placed it on the deck for her.

As the guys started eating, Davenport announced, "I got into trouble with my wife."

"What did you go and do this time, Jerry?" Parker asked.

"The other day, she asked me to hand her lipstick to her and I accidentally passed her a glue stick. She hasn't talked to me in a couple of days," Davenport joked.

"I'd like to borrow it," Kartheiser said with an all-knowing grin.

Layne leaned toward Parker and offered, "Matt, I want to give you a piece of advice about life."

"I'm waiting," Parker said as he and the others gave Layne their attention.

"I've always said that it's good to laugh." He paused before continuing, "Unless you have diarrhea."

The guys all laughed.

Layne looked at each one in turn before asking, "I guess none of you have it." He then chortled, and they joined in.

"Hey there," Layne began. "Earlier today I was thinking back to when I was in 8th grade – best three years of my life."

They all laughed aloud again and soon were finished eating. Davenport asked, "Ready to play euchre?"

"Deal them out," Kartheiser answered.

"I'm ready," Parker added. Davenport shuffled the cards and dealt five cards to each player.

Layne, who was seated to the left of Davenport, eyed the heart that was turned up and the cards in his hand. He stared at them longer than he should. He was confused.

"Are you going to pass or play, partner?" Parker asked. He was sitting directly across from Layne and patiently awaiting a response. He was eager to get on with the game.

"I think I'll pass," Layne replied.

The other two passed and Davenport picked up the heart and discarded another card. "Hearts are trump."

Smiling, Layne led off with the jack of clubs. "Okay boys. Let me have them."

"What do you mean, Zeke? My ace of clubs takes your jack," Kartheiser said as he laid his card on the table and the other two followed suit.

"What? I thought clubs were trump."

"I called hearts, Zeke," Davenport said in a kind tone. He and the others understood how the Alzheimer's was affecting Layne. They cared for their friend and tolerated his forgetfulness during their games.

"Great googly moogly! I didn't remember that," Layne said. He watched Kartheiser sweep the four played cards back to him.

"No harm," Kartheiser replied. He then led the jack of hearts, the highest trump card of the hand currently being played.

When it was Layne's turn to play a heart, he paused a moment as he looked at Kartheiser. "Ken, do you know the difference between playing euchre and arguing with your wife?"

The guys were always amazed at how Layne's memory worked when it came to jokes or one-liners.

"No," Kartheiser answered, although Layne told the same joke every time they played.

"You've at least a chance at winning when you play euchre," Layne laughed. He tossed a heart trump card on the pile.

Two hours later, Layne pushed back his chair and reached into his pocket. He pulled out his harmonica and looked at Jerry.

"Are you armed, Jerry?"

"Always," Davenport grinned. He produced his blues harp. "What do you want to start with?"

"How about *Train Whistle Blues?*"

"You got it," Davenport replied. The pair began to play. They followed it with *Lack of Luck, Island Bound, Aft End First* and *Our Old Lyman.*

When they finished, the other two applauded as did several people seated at nearby tables.

"Really enjoyed it," Parker said.

"Made the night complete," Kartheiser added.

The men decided to call it a night and headed for their vehicles.

"Zeke, can I give you a lift home?" Davenport asked.

"No," Layne said. He pointed across the Miller Ferry parking lot. "It's not that far. Sheba and I will take a slow walk home."

Davenport's eyes scanned the parking lot and didn't see anything that would cause him to protest. "Okay. Good night."

"Night," Layne said. Davenport climbed into his Jeep and headed home.

Shortly after midnight, Davenport was sleeping comfortably in his bed when the phone rang. He looked at his clock on the night stand as he answered the phone.

"Hello?"

"Jerry, it's Cathy. Is my dad with you?"

"No. He walked home after we finished playing euchre. Isn't he home?" Davenport asked as he began to worry.

"He isn't. I checked his room like I always do when I get home from work and he isn't there. I looked around and he wasn't on the deck either. Sheba is gone, too."

"I'll be right over. I'll meet you at the Catawba Inn and we can start looking for him," Davenport advised. He then quickly sat up and turned to look at his wife.

"What's wrong?" his wife, Cathy, asked.

"That was Cathy. Zeke is missing, I'm going to help her look for him," Davenport said. He arose from bed, quickly dressed and reached for his keys and wallet on the nightstand.

"Want me to come along?"

"I got this. He's probably lost and wandering around. I shouldn't be long," Davenport answered. He then headed out the door.

"Let me know if you need me to come up and help," she called.

"I will. Thanks, Hon."

Davenport departed and jumped into his glossy black Jeep Gladiator and drove off. He turned left on Northwest Catawba and raced to the Catawba Inn.

When he turned right on East Porter Street, he grabbed one of his West Marine LED spotlights from the floor and flashed its powerful 3,000 lumens as he drove slowly through the area. After he turned left on Crogan Street and drove past the Catawba Inn, he saw someone with a flashlight approaching him from the Miller Ferry parking lot. It was Cathy.

"Any sign of him?" he asked.

"No Jerry," she responded. The fear in her voice was obvious.

"Hop in." Davenport said.

When she jumped into the passenger seat, Davenport handed her his extra spotlight. "Here. Use this."

"Thanks, Jerry," she said. She took it and began shining it out her side of the vehicle. "How was Dad tonight?" she asked as they drove. "Anything unusual or of concern?"

"Nothing different from what we've all seen. Tonight, he couldn't remember where the restroom was. He made several misplays when we were playing cards. He couldn't remember, at times, which card was trump."

"I'm getting more and more concerned about him."

"Did you check on the ferry dock?"

"Yes. I walked down there and looked around. I called his name, but didn't see him anywhere. I also searched underneath the trailer and down on the rocks, but couldn't find him. I walked along Water Street, too."

"It's only about two blocks to your place from the Catawba Inn. I don't know how he could have got lost."

"That's my dad!"

They drove through the neighborhood and down Converse Street, Lawrence Drive and Buchanan Drive. As they made the turn on East Porter toward Route 53, Cathy shouted with relief. "There they are!"

Her light was directed to the entrance of the Catawba Island Historical Society Museum, which was the former Union Chapel. Sleeping on the sidewalk in front of the museum's entrance was Layne. Sheba woke and jumped to her feet, barking as the vehicle pulled to a stop.

"Quiet Sheba," Layne moaned. He cradled his head in his arms.

"Dad! What are you doing here?" Cathy asked, while leaping out of the Jeep.

"Minding my own business is what I'm doing. Why did you

wake me up?" he asked without opening his eyes.

"Do you know where you are?"

"In my bedroom. Where do you think I am?" He was perturbed at having his sleep disturbed. He had no idea that he wasn't at home.

"Zeke," Davenport started. He joined Cathy next to Layne. "You're lost. You're at the museum."

"Balderdash!" Layne said. He then opened his eyes and sat up. He turned and saw the museum door and turned back again to see his two rescuers. Not willing to admit his mistake, Layne said, "I'm just doing what people do the day after Thanksgiving. I'm sleeping in front of the door so I can be the first in tomorrow when they open."

"Nice try, Dad. But it's not working," Cathy responded.

"Let me help you up Zeke," Davenport said. He bent over and helped Layne to his feet. "Let's get you in the truck and I'll drive you home."

"If you must," Layne protested, but then went along with the suggestion.

As Davenport helped him into the front passenger seat, Cathy climbed in behind him.

"You'll be more comfortable in your own bed," Cathy said. She settled in and reached forward to pat her father's shoulder.

Layne responded with an incomprehensive mumble.

Several barks from Sheba announced that she spotted either a rabbit or squirrel. She took off after it.

"That dog can't resist those rabbits. She just goes nuts," Layne said in watching Sheba disappear around the side of the museum.

"She'll show up tomorrow on the back deck. She always does," he added.

"Let's get you home, Dad."

CHAPTER 4

The Layne Home
The Next Morning

Michelle walked into the kitchen where Cathy had just made breakfast.

"Hungry?"

"Yes, Mom."

"Here you go," Cathy said. She placed a plate of bacon and eggs on the counter for Michelle, who then sat on one of the stools and started to eat.

Michelle looked at her mother's face and noticed she displayed a distant look.

"What's wrong, Mom?"

Cathy set her fork on her plate and turned to look at her caring daughter. Unable to control herself, she started to sob.

"What's wrong, Mom?" Michelle asked. She scooted her stool closer to her mother and placed her arm around her to comfort her.

"Did something happen at work?"

"No," Cathy sobbed.

"What is it then? You can tell me," Michelle urged her in a quiet tone.

"It's your grandfather."

"What did he do now?"

Cathy explained the events from the previous night.

"Oh no. Is he okay?"

"I guess so. I checked his room when I got up and he was gone. I see his cereal bowl and coffee cup in the sink. Sheba's gone. I bet they're already down at the ferry dock."

"I'll check before I go to work," Michelle said. She turned back to her breakfast.

"Give him a hug. You know how he likes hugs," Cathy suggested.

"I will," Michelle said. She stood and took her dirty plate to the sink. "I'll go now and see. Then I'll see you at work, right?"

Besides their regular jobs, they each worked a few hours a week at the Waterline Gift Shop next to the mobile home.

"Yes," Cathy said as she poked at her eggs.

"Are you sure that you're okay, Mom?"

"I'll be all right. Go along and I'll see you at the Waterline."

"Okay."

Michelle left and walked down to the ferry dock. She spied her grandfather in the waiting room. Sheba was at his side as he talked to several children who were waiting to board the next ferry for South Bass Island.

"Suddenly he pointed up in the sky. "Look! There's a dead seagull!"

As the children looked up, he started laughing.

"The old flying dead seagull prank, huh Grandpa?" Michelle asked as she neared him.

Layne chuckled and so did the children as they realized they had been pranked.

"Don't you have to be at work?"

"I'm on my way. I just wanted to give you a hug before I

started." She wrapped her arms around Layne. "I want you to know that I love you, Grandpa."

Layne patted her arm. "I know you do, Princess. I know you do."

Releasing her hug, she said, "I better go."

"You have yourself a good day," Layne said. She turned and walked away.

Michelle abruptly stopped, then turned back toward Layne and called, "Grandpa, it looks like that man is having trouble with his car."

Layne turned and looked in the direction she was pointing. In the line of vehicles waiting to drive onto the next ferry, he saw a midnight blue Porsche 4S Carrera Cabriolet. The hood to the rear engine was raised. Its tall, muscular driver with graying hair was impeccably attired in resort wear. He was curiously peering into the engine compartment.

"Maybe I can help," Layne suggested. He followed his granddaughter into the vehicle lanes.

As they neared the car, an attractive brown-haired woman wearing dark sunglasses slid out of the passenger seat and joined her companion at the rear of the car.

"What do you think the problem is? Starter? Battery?" she asked.

"Battery," acknowledged the driver. The man appeared to be in his fifties. He had an air of sophistication about him with a suggestive touch of danger. Not someone to be messed with.

"Maybe I can help you," Layne offered. He approached and stood next to the car. He pulled on his red suspenders and let them snap against his chest. He eyed the man who seemed as suave as James Bond. The gorgeous woman, Layne mused, could be a Bond girl with ease.

The driver grinned as he gently teased Layne. "Not sure that those suspenders can do the work of jumper cables." He stuck out his hand. "I'm Randy Lowry and this is Suzanne Carlson," he said, in introducing himself and his passenger.

"Nice to meet you both. I'm Zeke Layne and this pretty redhead is my granddaughter, Michelle," Layne said. He shook Lowry's hand. "Headed to Put-in-Bay, I see."

"We were until this happened. We had planned on doing a day trip and having some island wine."

"It's a good thing I happened to be here," Layne said as he looked at the vehicles waiting in line. "I can help solve your dilemma."

"Wonderful," Carlson said with a warm smile. "It's a dead battery," she added.

"Do you know Mad Dog Adams?" Layne asked.

"No, we don't know him, but we've heard about him. He entertains at the Round House, doesn't he?" Lowry asked.

"He does and he's going to help you out of your problem. He's sitting in that truck in the next lane and I'd guess in a perfect position to pop his hood and jump your battery." Layne waved at Adams to get his attention. "Hey Mike, do you have any jumper cables?"

The burly entertainer, who was wearing a stars and stripes dew rag and a white denim shirt with the sleeves cut off, smiled from his front seat. He leaned toward the open passenger window. "Need a little help in bringing that baby back to life?"

"We do," Lowry replied as he looked at Adams.

"We can get you fixed right up. I've got a pair of jumper cables in the back."

"I just knew that you'd have a set of jumper cables," Layne smiled.

"Always have them. I never know when I need a little jolt of creativity and need to hook them up to myself," Adams teased. He exited his truck and grabbed the cables.

Within minutes, they had the cables connected to the Carrera's battery in the front trunk compartment and started Lowry's Porsche. Adams unclamped the cables and closed the car hood just as the vehicles ahead began to move toward the boarding ramp.

"Thank you very much, Mike," Lowry said. He handed Adams and Layne a business card. "If you ever need any advice, give me a call. I owe you one."

"A lawyer. I should have known by the way you carried yourself," Layne remarked. He inserted the card in his wallet.

"Might just do that. Stop by the Round House this afternoon and catch my show. I can have your lady friend come up on the stage with me and blow the conch. It's part of the show," Adams urged.

"I don't know," a hesitant Carlson said from the passenger seat.

"It will be fun." Adams saw Parker waving for the Porsche to board and turned back to Lowry. "They're waving you forward. You better go."

Lowry put the car in gear and began moving forward. "Thanks again, guys," he said as he headed toward Parker to hand him his ferry tickets and drive aboard.

"Thanks for helping out, Mike," Layne said. Adams returned to his vehicle as it was his turn to drive on board the ferry.

"No problem. I used them the other day to jump start a lady's cell phone," he teased, then drove away.

Michelle hurried away to her job while Layne returned to the passenger waiting shelter.

CHAPTER 5

The Layne Home
The Next Morning

"Dad, we're having company today," Cathy announced.

"We are? Who's coming?"

"My stepsisters."

"Where's my phone. I need to make an emergency call."

"What do you mean, Dad?"

"I need to call an exterminator over here real quick like. He can spray before they get here, and they won't invade our home." He wasn't teasing. He didn't like them around because they usually showed up when they wanted money.

Cathy didn't like them around either, but she did her best to be gracious. "Look at the bright side, Dad."

"Bright side? What bright side? All I've ever seen with those two harlots is the dark side," he grumbled.

"The good news is they live in Toledo," she said in trying to put on a positive spin on her little heads-up.

"The South Pole isn't far enough away for me," he cracked. "When are they going to be here so I know when to disappear?"

"Dad."

"Dad what?"

"Be nice."

"I would if there was a good reason," Layne countered. "They're twin sisters and they can't remember each other's birthday. How stupid is that?"

"They're just a little different."

"The Doomsday Twins is what I call them. No, the harbingers of doom is better."

Before they could continue, the sound of car doors slamming interrupted them. Cathy walked over to the front door and looked out. "What a surprise! They're early."

"When did they get doors on the brooms they rode over here?" Layne asked. He then headed for the back door to the deck to escape, but didn't get far.

"Dad, don't," Cathy firmly said in a tone that meant business.

Layne retraced his steps and plopped into the sofa. "Tell Liver Lips and Frostbite that I'm napping," he said. He then shuttered his eyes.

Cathy opened the door and greeted her stepsisters. "Hello Blair. Hi Ida. How nice to see you two."

"Hi Cathy. Where's your dad?" Blair asked as she got to the point. She was on a mission.

Before Cathy could answer, Ida fanned her red face and declared, "It was so hot in the car. The air conditioner doesn't work."

"Neither do your brains," Layne muttered under his breath.

"Why didn't you drive over in your car, Ida?" Cathy asked.

"It needs a new transmission."

"It wouldn't if you wouldn't drive like a maniac!" Blair snapped at her sister.

This sounds expensive and probably why they are here, Layne thought.

"Has he been sleeping long?" Blair asked. She walked over to Layne.

"Not very," Cathy replied.

Blair stuck out her foot and gave the sofa a hard kick. "Wake up. You've got company," she said in a high-pitched voice.

"Oh no. That's not how you treat our handsome stepfather," Ida cooed. She rushed past Blair and placed a protective arm around Layne's shoulders while he opened his eyes.

"You girls get lost and end up here?" he asked. As Ida walked to the kitchen and opened the fridge, Layne suggested cynically, "Just help yourself to anything."

"Got any cold beer?"

Cathy, being the good hostess that she was, replied, "Yes. Help yourselves to a cold one. Blair, would you like a beer?"

"Yes. Make it two," she said. She then dropped upon the sofa next to Layne. "That will save you an extra trip when you bring them to me." Blair turned her attention to Layne. "What have you been up to old-timer?"

"Nothing. Just spending time over at the ferry dock. I don't go anywhere."

"I bet you couldn't remember if you did go anywhere," Ida cracked. She took another a swig on her beer.

"Here's your two beers, Blair," Cathy said. She set them on the coffee table.

"Thanks." She turned her face toward Layne as she reached for one of the open beer bottles. "I hope you haven't been traveling a lot. You know you'd be burning up the inheritance money that our momma promised you had for us."

"There's not much there," Layne explained. "Your momma always thought there was a lot." There actually was a modest amount since Layne had been such a thrifty saver, but he wasn't going to let them know.

"Morning Mom," Michelle said, while walking into the kitchen. When she saw the visitors, she wished she had stayed in her room until they had gone. Like her mother, she greeted them graciously. "Hi Aunt Blair. Hi Aunt Ida."

The two aunts eyed Cathy's beautiful daughter. They were jealous of her good looks.

"You feeling alright? You putting on weight?" Blair asked.

"Are you pregnant?" Ida snickered in a mean tone.

Michelle spun on her heels and went back to her room.

"That was really uncalled for," Cathy said at the cruel comments.

"Oh, we were just teasing her," Ida countered. "I need to use your bathroom."

"It's down the hall."

Ida walked away as Blair finished emptying her first beer. Looking at Layne, she asked, "Have things have been a bit tight?"

"Like a pig's butt in fly season?" Layne quipped.

Blair suppressed snapping back at Layne. "What a clever comment," she said as she began to work on Layne. "Things have been tough on us, too. Ida got laid off. I'm behind two months' rent."

"You two can't find work?"

"No one wants to hire us. We're on unemployment and food stamps."

"Must be the background checks that are working against you. You both have been fired for stealing as I recall," Layne said. He was proud that his memory presently seemed to be firing on all cylinders.

"Those were lies. Those companies had it in for us," Blair

retorted.

"Well, things have been tight around here, too." Layne was in no mood to give any money to the two leeches.

Ida walked back into the kitchen. "Your bathroom floor is wet." She looked at Layne. "Did you pee on the floor?"

Cathy stepped in to defend her father. "He has accidents sometimes. I'll clean it right up." She hurried to the bathroom.

"Better you than me. I don't clean up after anyone," Ida barked.

"It's a good thing you don't have kids," Layne cracked back. "They wouldn't get their diapers changed if you have that kind of attitude."

"That's right and I wouldn't change your Depends either," Ida snarled.

"Great googly moogly! This is going downhill fast," Layne said. He felt his temper rising.

Ida threw a wink at Blair. "Let's get out of here. We're not welcome."

"I believe that's the smartest thing I've heard you say in a long time," Layne smiled.

"I'm taking my beer with me," Blair said. She arose to her feet and declared, "We're out of here."

Layne was so pleased they were leaving that he couldn't help himself. He reached into his wallet and pulled out a fifty-dollar bill. "Here. I'll at least help you with gas money," he said. He handed the money to Blair.

Blair looked at the bill in her hand. "My momma would have given us more." She turned on her heels and followed Ida out the door.

When they got into Blair's car, Ida complained, "It's so hot. Turn on the air conditioner."

Blair reached down and turned on the supposedly nonworking air conditioner which began to immediately cool the car's interior. "Did you find anything?"

"I went straight to his bedroom before I went into the bathroom. I looked through his nightstand drawers and his dresser drawers. "Look what I found!"

As they drove away, Blair glanced at the wad of cash in Ida's hand. "How much did you get?"

"Three hundred dollars," she grinned. "I found it hidden in the back of his sock drawer."

"He's getting so forgetful I bet he won't realize that it's missing."

"I hope so. Party time!" Ida cackled.

Inside the trailer, Layne stood from his chair. "I'm glad they're gone. They wear on me."

"I know what you mean, Dad."

Layne walked over to the kitchen cabinets and opened one. "Great googly moogly! Irish Gin's carrots are gone. I bet they stole them," he said. He then angrily shut the cabinet.

"Dad, we never keep carrots in the cabinet. They're in the fridge," she said with concern. "Let me get them for you and put them in a bag."

"Okay. I'm going to get my cap. I'll be right back."

He returned within two minutes and was wearing his cap as she handed him a bag with the carrots.

"I'm going to head to the ferry dock and stop to see Irish Gin before I come home. She needs her carrots."

"Have fun," Cathy called. Layne walked out the front door with Sheba at his side.

CHAPTER 6

The Layne Home
That Evening

Layne was watching TV and rubbing Sheba's neck when he saw a van pull up in front of the trailer. He heard Michelle answer her cell phone down the hall. When he looked toward her, his eyes popped. She was dressed in a miniskirt and low-cut top.

"Where do you think you're going dressed like that? Your lungs are falling out of that top," Layne asked with concern.

"I have a date. We're going to a drive-in movie."

"You're not going anywhere dressed like that," Layne fumed.

"Grandpa," she pleaded.

"No way. Don't even think twice. If you want to go, you go and change into a pair of jeans and a normal top. And no buttons down the front. Wear a tee shirt or something like that," Layne ordered.

"But Grandpa."

"Go on now. Do as I say. I'm going out to meet this boy."

"He's not exactly a boy," she stammered.

"How old is he?"

"Twenty-two. He belongs to one of the yacht clubs."

"He's too old for you."

"No, he isn't. Some of my friends are dating guys that old."

"How did you meet him?"

"At the Dairy Dock."

"You go change."

"Grandpa!"

"Go on now."

Reluctantly, Michelle turned and walked back to her room. Layne walked outside.

"You here for Michelle?" he asked the young man, who looked like his parents had money to burn.

"Yes. I'm Connor Palmer," he said with an air of sophistication. "You must be Michelle's grandfather. I'm pleased to meet you, sir," he said, while extending his hand.

This guy reminds me of a snobby kid like Eddie Haskell on the *Leave It To Beaver* TV show, Layne thought to himself.

"Going to the drive-in, huh?" Layne asked as he shook the hand.

"Yes. In Monroeville."

"I remember those days. Taking a date to the drive-in can be fun, you know what I mean?" He gave Palmer a sly wink.

The boy smiled. "Yes, I do," he replied with a conspiratorial look.

"Mind if I look inside, Connor?"

"Go ahead," Palmer replied. He slid open the side door. "I like your red suspenders."

"So do I. Thank you. Very nice. You've got a nice bed back here. Good to have for camping trips."

"It is," Palmer quickly agreed. "Always need to be prepared," he said. He gave Layne a boyish, almost devilish wink of the eye.

"Got any beer, young man?"

Palmer pointed to a cooler between the front bucket seats.

"Armed and dangerous, huh?"

"What are you two talking about?" Michelle asked as she emerged in a more modest outfit from the trailer. She joined the two men at the van.

"Your friend was showing me how well equipped the van is for going to a drive-in." Layne turned to Palmer. "Don't go yet. I want to go inside and get you something that you're missing."

Michelle had a perplexed look on her face as Layne walked inside.

"Your grandfather seems like a cool dude," Palmer remarked.

"Oh, he's a handful," Michelle admitted.

"I'm serious."

"Cool beans," she smiled. "There's no one quite like my grandpa," she added.

A couple of minutes later, Layne emerged from the house. He was wearing his cap and carrying a bag. Sheba followed him.

"Grandpa, what are you doing?"

"I'm coming with you," he said. He climbed into the van and sat on the bed. "I haven't been to a drive-in in years. I brought my own chips and a candy bar. Come on Sheba. Jump in here."

Sheba jumped into the van as Michelle turned to Palmer. "I'm really sorry about this. If you want to cancel our date, I understand."

Palmer looked at Layne and the panting dog. "Nah. I bet they both fall asleep within an hour. We can still do this," he said confidently as he slid the door closed. He opened the passenger door so Michelle could enter, then walked around to his door. Within a minute, the van pulled away.

The next morning, Michelle found her mother in the kitchen.

"How did your date go last night? You went to a movie, right?" Cathy continued cooking scrambled eggs.

"The drive-in."

"I didn't realize you were going to a drive-in," Cathy said. A worried look appeared on her face.

"No worry. Grandpa went with us."

"What?"

"So did Sheba."

"I didn't know they were invited."

"They invited themselves."

"Did you have a nice time?"

"Not really."

"What do you mean?"

"Grandpa fell asleep while we were still driving to Monroeville."

"Oh dear, he was tired out from that visit with your aunts. I'm sure that drained him."

"And Sheba decided that she was going to sit on the cooler between the front seats. Any time that Connor would reach down to open the cooler, she'd growl at him. So, we didn't get any of the cold drinks that we brought with us."

Cathy chuckled softly as she visualized the situation.

"On top of that, Sheba wanted to lick my face almost the whole time. We didn't stay for the second movie. Connor said he had a headache and brought me home early."

"Is he going to ask you out on another date?"

"I don't think so. I think he was mad."

"Did he say anything?"

"No, but he peeled out of here when he left last night. He dropped us off and took off," Michelle explained. She paused for a moment before continuing. "Mom, Grandpa was confused last night."

"People can be when they wake up."

"No. When we got out of the van, he started walking to the ferry dock. I asked him where he was going, and he said to his bedroom. I had to grab him by the hand, bring him inside the trailer and take him down the hall."

Cathy wrinkled her brow as she thought. "That is concerning."

"Where is he now?"

"Down at the ferry dock, playing to his fans. We just need to keep a closer eye on him," Cathy advised. She thought back to him being lost after the recent euchre game and concluded his condition continued to deteriorate.

CHAPTER 7

Arbors Nursing Home
The Next Morning

Cathy drove Layne to Sandusky so he could visit an old friend, Lonnie Morris. The men once worked together for some years aboard the Miller ferry and had developed a strong friendship. Sadly, Morris' Alzheimer's disease had worsened and his medical prognosis was grim.

Cathy and her dad checked in at the front desk. They were buzzed through the locked doors to enter the section where Morris lived. They found his room and Layne knocked at the door.

"Lonnie? Okay to come in?"

"Who is it?" Morris asked.

"It's me, Zeke."

"I don't know who you are. I'm not buying anything today. Go away."

Ignoring the response, Layne slowly led Cathy into the room where they saw Morris sitting in a chair. His breakfast was on a wheeled table in front of him. His appearance was disheveled and his head was lowered as if he were staring at the floor.

"Lonnie, now do you know who I am?" Layne asked. He did his best to smile even though he was shocked every time he saw his friend. The once mountainous, take-on-anybody ruf-fian, had become a wasted and frightened old man. "Lonnie? Hey, pal."

"Come closer so I can see you better," Morris weakly urged. He raised his head then squinted his eyes to look over his visitor.

"It's Zeke."

Morris stared at him for another minute. "How do I know you?"

"We worked together on the Miller Ferry."

Morris turned his attention back to his food. His hand shook so bad that he used a weighted spoon to help hold his food.

Layne and Cathy watched while he finished the last two bites of his cereal and an aide appeared to take away his bowl.

Morris stared at Layne. "What did you say your name was?"

"Zeke Layne. I live over at the Catawba Ferry Dock. We worked together on the ferry."

Morris looked down at the table in front of him and his eyes widened. "Somebody stole my bowl. I was eating breakfast and they stole my bowl. Did you take my bowl?" he asked as he eyed Layne.

"The nurse's aide came in and took your dish. You had fin-ished eating, Lonnie," Cathy explained in a calm voice.

"Who are you?"

"I'm Zeke's daughter. I use to bother you when you visited our house to play cards with my dad."

"Who's your dad?"

"Zeke Layne. He's right here next to me."

Morris continued as if the exchange hadn't happened. "The aides steal things here. My things. See. You can't let your guard down for a second. I'm going to call the police."

Morris looked for a phone and didn't see one in his sparse room. "Now they stole the phone. Will you call them for me?" he asked. He looked at Layne.

"I'll be glad to call them for you."

Layne was becoming very depressed at seeing the additional deterioration in his friend. It was frustrating not being able to carry on a coherent conversation. He also suspected from time to time that he too, might one day end up in a similar condition.

"I don't like this hotel anymore. I think I'll check out. You tell the front desk that I'm leaving today." Morris looked around the room. "I don't remember my room number. Just give them my name."

"I'll do that," Layne said. He reached up to his right eye and wiped away a tear.

Cathy noticed the movement and also the emotional stress that Layne was going through. "Dad, we should go now."

"I guess we should." Layne walked over to Morris and patted his shoulder. "We're going to leave now."

Morris pulled back. "Who are you?"

Speaking softly, Layne answered, "I'm one of your best friends, Zeke Layne, and I will always be one of your best friends."

Morris seemed oblivious to the answer as he looked down at his table. "Somebody stole my bowl."

Cathy gently grabbed her father's arm and walked him to the doorway. "It was nice seeing you, Lonnie."

They returned to the car and headed back to Catawba.

Cathy glanced at her father as she drove. He was slumped in his seat. His eyes had lost their sparkle. He seemed forlorn after the visit. She was also stunned by the degradation she had seen in Lonnie. She couldn't imagine the great impact it had on her father, seeing his dear friend in that sad state.

"Dad, are you okay?"

Layne didn't respond right away. He looked out of his window as they rode up the entrance ramp to Route 2.

"Yes," he mumbled quietly, although he didn't feel that way. Fear filled him as he again thought about his own condition. He didn't want to advance to the state that Morris was in. "I'm just fine," he added, unconvincingly.

She decided to allow him to have his quiet time to reflect. When they reached the trailer, she parked her car and they went inside.

"Would you like me to make you lunch before you go down to the ferry dock?"

"Sure, but I don't think I'll go to the dock today. I'm just going outside and sit on the deck," he said in a morose tone.

"I'll make an egg salad sandwich for you."

"That'll be fine," Layne said. He opened the slider and walked onto the deck. He settled into a chair and smiled when he saw Sheba climbing the steps. She went to her water dish and lapped water before taking her normal position on the deck floor next to Layne.

Layne reached down and rubbed her head. "What would I do without you, Sheba?" He smiled for the first time in the last several hours. He was frustrated at not being able to help his friend and what he would face as his own condition worsened.

The slider opened and Cathy emerged with his sandwich and a cold bottle of beer. "Here you go, Dad," she said. She set them down on a small table next to his chair. She then walked behind her father and began rubbing his shoulders.

"I'm sorry about your friend."

"Yeah. I am, too. Cathy?"

"Yes."

"I want you to promise me one thing."

"Anything, Dad."

"If I get in that condition, I don't want you to put me in one of those homes. I want to stay here where I can watch the lake and the ferry boats coming and going. Will you promise me that?"

"I promise, Dad," Cathy replied in a firm voice that echoed her commitment. "I won't abandon you like I was abandoned by the person I trusted the most."

"You mean that stupid husband of yours?"

"Yes. I want you to know that I'm not going to abandon you," she reassured him.

"Thank you, Honey." Layne reached up and gently patted her hand. "I never did like that husband of yours."

"We all make mistakes," she observed.

"Yeah, like I did with your stepmother. I never should have married her, especially after I met her doomsday twins."

"Dad, do you remember when I was growing up and I was afraid of lake monsters under my bed?"

That memory triggered a large smile on Layne's face. "I do, Honey."

"You'd come in and calm me down. You'd climb in bed with me and lay there, telling me that you wouldn't let any lake monsters harm me."

Layne chuckled. "I do, and I told you that I was your knight in shining armor and I'd always rescue you."

"That's right. Dad, I'll always be there for you and rescue you. Don't you worry about what tomorrow brings. I'm there for you." Cathy bent over and gave her father a kiss on the cheek.

"Thank you, Honey. You and Michelle have a way of bringing joy into my life and chasing away my fears."

"It's my turn to do that, Dad," she said, while rubbing her cheek against his cheek. "Do you want to come in?"

"No. I think I'll just sit out here and count my blessings this afternoon. Right, Sheba?"

Hearing her name, Sheba barked twice.

Cathy went inside the house as Layne reached for his sandwich.

CHAPTER 8

The Layne Home
A Few Days Later

The roaring of two motorcycle engines in front of the trailer interrupted Layne's peaceful lunch.

"What in the world!" he exclaimed. He looked from the kitchen counter toward one of the front windows.

Cathy moved quickly to look outside. "Dad, you're not going to believe this."

"I'm fastening my seat belt so I don't fall off this stool. What is it?"

"I think it's Ida and two bikers. We're having a surprise visit."

"I'd say it's more like an invasion. I'll get out the bug repellant. Maybe they'll go away," he suggested. Layne arose from the stool. "Let's go outside so they won't come in."

"Dad!"

Layne barged right past her and walked outside to where Ida was dismounting from the back of one of the bikes.

"Hi Zeke," she smiled. She slipped off her helmet. Neither of the two other bikers wore a helmet.

"Meet my friends. This is my new boyfriend, Bonehead." Ida next introduced the rider with greasy black hair that was pulled back in a sweaty ponytail. He had a red bandana around his head and wore mirrored aviator sunglasses. He had a scraggly beard and a hooked nose.

"Bonehead, this is my stepsister, Cathy, and my stepfather, Zeke."

"Nice to meet you, Dumbhead," Layne said sarcastically.

"It's Bonehead. That's my biker name, old man," Bonehead said in a dangerous tone. He had a mean streak to him. It seethed just below the surface of his skin.

Ida ignored the exchange as she continued to introduce the second biker. "This is Guardrail."

"That's a stupid name," Layne said. He wasn't one to hold back, especially with intruders like these.

"He got that moniker after crashing into a guardrail on one of his bikes," Bonehead snarled with an upturned upper lip.

"I got me a biker name, too. You shouldn't call me Ida anymore. It's Siren," Ida said proudly.

"Siren? It sounds like a stripper's name."

"Oh Zeke, you are so funny," Ida retorted.

A compliment, Layne thought. She must want money. "Did you meet Hammerhead at the unemployment office?"

"Bonehead, Zeke," Ida corrected him. "Oh no. I met him a few days ago. He was riding down the street and just couldn't resist stopping to talk to a pretty girl like me. Isn't that right, Bonehead?"

"Yeah. Something like that," Bonehead said. He brushed off his leather vest. When he turned around, Layne saw that it had his biker club logo. It was the name October Brotherhood encircling a naked mermaid positioned in the center.

"Bonehead is a machinist at the Jeep factory in south Toledo. He's got a real good job. Tell him about your bike, Bonehead," she encouraged him.

Bonehead slid his glasses off his face onto the top of his head. "It's a 1958 Harley-Davidson Panhead Duo-Glide. I added a jockey shifter and foot-mounted suicide clutch. She's got a 74-cubic inch V-twin, air-cooled motor mounted in a stretch frame. I added an electric-start kit with a custom seat and Avon Speedmaster Mark II tires. Like the color?"

"Nice," Layne couldn't help himself.

"That's the original Calypso Red and Birch White two-tone paint scheme."

"Bonehead is going to have my face painted on the tank with my name under it so he'll think of me whenever he is riding it," Ida said proudly. "It will be my biker name, Siren," she added quickly.

"Doesn't anyone want to know about my bike?" Guardrail asked. He wore black sunglasses and had gray hair and a long mustache with a goatee. When he spoke, he showed that he was missing his two front teeth.

"Go ahead," Layne said, thinking he could hear the wind whistling between Guardrail's ears. He turned to look at the black bike with gold pinstriping.

"My bike is a 1978 FLHS Harley-Davidson Electra-Glide with an 80-cubic inch V-twin Shovelhead engine. She's chain-driven and she has front and rear disc brakes. You can see her Dunlop whitewall tires and chromed straight drag pipes. My Mustang solo seat has tassels."

"Like a stripper. I'm surprised that, Siren, you didn't bring your tassels." Layne couldn't help himself.

No one laughed.

"You work with Dumbhead?" Layne asked.

"It's Bonehead," Bonehead snarled at Layne.

It was apparent that neither liked the other.

"No, I fuel aircraft at Toledo Express Airport," Guardrail answered.

Layne made a mental note that he would never take a flight out of that airport. He sensed that Guardrail wasn't all there. You could give him a baseball bat and tell him that a hornet's nest was a pinata – and he'd go swing at it.

"You all must be thirsty after your ride from Toledo. Why don't you come in and freshen up?" Cathy offered.

Layne frowned at her invitation. He didn't want them in his home.

"Sounds good to me," Bonehead said. He surged past everyone and walked into the trailer. He headed to the fridge and opened the door as if he owned the place. He reached in and withdrew three beers before kicking the fridge door shut behind him. He handed one to Ida and Guardrail before plopping into Layne's easy chair and popping his can open.

"I guess I don't need to tell you to make yourself at home," Layne grumbled, while walking into his trailer.

"Dad, be nice," Cathy cautioned Layne.

"I am," Layne grumbled softly.

Guardrail sat on the sofa while Ida stood next to the kitchen counter.

"Is that piece of rusted junk out there, your pickup truck?" Bonehead asked as he looked at Layne.

"Yes," Layne replied.

"I bet she'd do zero to sixty in an hour depending on how fast you could pedal. Right old man?" Bonehead laughed sarcastically.

Guardrail laughed as if on cue.

Layne didn't answer his rude question. Instead, he commented in a serious tone as he looked at Bonehead's hair which was tied back in a ponytail, "Life is kind of funny. You don't always know what to expect. But one thing I do know is that if I lift a ponytail, I'll always find a horse's ass."

"Dad! That wasn't a nice comment," Cathy interjected.

"Neither was his," Layne countered. He looked at Bonehead, and Bonehead's dark eyes narrowed. They were cold and rigid.

"You be nice to my man, Zeke," Ida stormed. "He's HIV positive," she blurted out without thinking.

"Siren! Shut up!" Bonehead screamed. His face instantly turned red with rage.

"He got it from a needle," Ida added hurriedly.

"I told you to shut up! You want me to have Guardrail slap you into the next county?" Her words were fueling the ugly fire that burned within him.

Cathy tried to calm down the situation. "What brings you to Catawba?" Cathy asked Ida.

"We were out for a ride and I told Bonehead that I wanted him to meet the family."

"Getting real serious, huh? After meeting a few days ago?" Layne mumbled. She's not very picky, Layne thought.

"Oh, he just rocks my world," Ida exclaimed excitedly.

Layne eyed Ida's face. "Ida, you need to trim that mustache you got growing!"

Ida's eyes bulged out in indignation as her hand went to her upper lip.

"Dad!" Cathy again cautioned Layne.

"Okay. I shouldn't have said it. But she looks like she's ready to walk the green mile," he chuckled quietly.

"Dad!"

"How old are you?" Bonehead asked Layne. He was trying to size up the old man.

"Old enough," Layne replied. He was getting weary of his visitors.

"I knew you were old when I first saw you. It's easy to tell if a man is old. It's when they start hiking their pants up to their nipples," he roared. Ida and Guardrail joined in the laughter. "That's probably why you wear those red suspenders!"

Layne started to fume. He decided he better leave before he erupted. "I'm going outside," Layne said. He inattentively opened the closet door. Realizing it wasn't the door to the deck, he closed it and opened the slider, quickly leaving the room. He had his fill of the rowdy visitors.

Bonehead couldn't quit. He stood and walked out on the deck where Layne was petting Sheba. Spotting Bonehead, Sheba let out a growl. She didn't like Bonehead. She sensed he was bad news.

"Smart dog," Layne grinned. He rubbed her head between her ears.

Bonehead backed up against the slider. "Does she bite?" he asked cautiously.

Layne was enjoying the moment. He decided to have a little fun at the expense of his unwanted visitor.

"Not usually. Just make sure she doesn't know what you were riding when you came here," Layne cautioned.

"You mean my..."

Layne abruptly stopped him from saying motorcycle. "Don't say it. She's a smart dog. If she knows that's yours, she'll tear into you."

"Oh sure," Bonehead said. He wasn't sure if he was buying the explanation.

"Oh, it's true. Goes back a year when one tried to run her over as he slowed down to make the curve out front. He wasn't wearing a helmet and she launched herself at his head. She tore the man's face in a jagged line across the cheek. His top lip was hanging off. Blood everywhere," Layne said as he continued with his tall tale.

Bonehead carefully glanced at the dog who returned it with a snarl. "Dogs are okay," he said. He tried to appear nonchalant about the situation. "You catch any fish here?" Bonehead asked, while looking from the rocks below out to the lake.

"Sometimes."

"I bet fish just tremble when they hear your name," Bonehead said sarcastically.

"I suppose just like women tremble when you walk into a room," Layne scoffed back.

Bonehead took a last look at the dog and Layne, then turned on his heels and walked inside.

"What do we have here?" Bonehead asked. He dropped back into the easy chair as he saw Michelle enter the room.

"I heard voices, Mom," she said as she walked up to her mother.

"Ida brought her friends over for a visit. This is Bonehead and Guardrail."

"Hi," Michelle smiled even though she was immediately uncomfortable with the two men.

"Hello there, Sweet Britches. Come on over here and sit on my lap," Bonehead suggested. He allowed his eyes to roam over her young body.

"No, I don't think so."

"I'd appreciate it if you didn't talk or look at my daughter that way, Bonehead," Cathy advised sternly.

"No offense intended. I was just teasing her."

"I'm going to use the bathroom," Ida said. She started walking down the hall.

When Cathy saw her walk into Layne's bedroom, she hurried down the hall. "Ida, are you lost?" Cathy walked into the bedroom and saw Ida quickly shut one of her dad's dresser drawers. "What are you doing?"

"I was looking for a hairband."

"In my dad's room? You're not going to find one here. Come on down to the bathroom and I'll give you one."

"Okay," Ida replied, embarrassed at being caught.

Meanwhile, Bonehead stood and walked over to Michelle. He placed his arm around her waist and pulled her against his side. "You sure are a cute little thing. I think I should trade in Ida for you."

"Fat chance!" Michelle said, while forcefully pulling away.

Bonehead followed her to the counter. He wasn't giving up so easily. He placed his hand on her lower back and allowed it to slip to the top of her backside. "Aw come on, Sweet Britches. You know you want me," he leered.

Michelle deftly twirled around and lashed out with her right foot. It connected with his shin, causing him to grunt in pain. She strode across the room and went outside to be with her grandfather.

When Cathy and Ida returned to the room, Guardrail was still chuckling at the pain Michelle had caused to Bonehead's shin.

"What's so funny?" Ida asked.

"Nothing. I'm ready to go," Bonehead said. He took the last gulp of beer in the can and threw it to the floor. Guardrail quickly drank the rest of his beer.

"I haven't finished my beer yet," Ida whined.

"Siren, I'm leaving now, with you or without you," Bonehead said, before he and Guardrail walked out the door.

Ida followed quickly. When they heard the bike engines roar to life, Layne and Michelle walked around the trailer to the front of the house. Sheba tagged along.

They stopped at the front corner and Layne bent down to talk to Sheba. "See them two bikers. If you ever see them again, you have my permission to bite them."

"And mine," Michelle chimed in.

Sheba barked. She then saw a rabbit across the road and suddenly sprinted after it, causing an approaching car to slam on its brakes to avoid hitting her.

"Sorry folks," Layne said to the car's driver. "She goes crazy when she sees a rabbit."

"No problem," the driver said as he continued on his way.

"That dog is going to cause an accident one of these days," Layne said. They watched their biker visitors roar away. "Let's go inside and talk to your mother. I want you to tell her what Bumblehead did to you."

Michelle smiled at Layne and took his hand as they walked into the front of the trailer.

As they entered, Cathy said, "That was certainly an interesting visit."

"That crackhead must have got a day pass from jail so he could bother us," Layne grumbled. "Michelle, tell your mother what he did to you."

Michelle gave her a quick recap. "He creeps me out, Mom. I don't want to be around him."

"You don't have anything to worry about, Honey. They live a long way from here. Besides, your grandfather and I will protect you."

"And my two friends, Mr. Smith and Mr. Wesson, are waiting in my bedroom in case there's any trouble with those two hooligans," Layne added.

What he didn't know was that Cathy had taken the rounds out of the revolver and hidden them so that Layne wouldn't hurt himself or anyone else.

"I just don't like him." Michelle wasn't stopping.

"I don't blame you, Michelle. That shidiot is not right. Makes me wonder if a horse kicked him in the head when he was a kid."

"Dad," Cathy said in a calm voice. "Both of you. They're gone. Let's just enjoy the day before Michelle and I have to go to work."

Michelle rolled her eyes and went down the hall to her room. Layne followed her although he went to his bedroom. When he emerged, he was wearing his cap.

"I'm heading down to the ferry dock. At least I'm appreciated there.

"Take your carrots. You're still going over to see Irish Gin today, right?"

"Yes," he said as he took the carrots and walked out the front door. "Sheba. Sheba," Layne called out. He looked across the street for his dog. Not seeing her, he headed down to the ferry dock.

CHAPTER 9

The Layne Home
The Next Day

"Dad, I'm running into Port Clinton to pick up a prescription. Do you need anything?"

"Bullets."

"What do you mean bullets?" Cathy asked as she feigned ignorance.

"I checked my revolver last night and somebody stole the bullets out of it. I know it was loaded the last time I checked."

Nodding her head, Cathy said, "I'll see if I can find some. It's a .38, right?" She had no intention of buying any, but played along as she heard him looking through his dresser drawers.

"I thought I hid some extras in here. I don't know. I can't find anything and I don't remember where I put stuff. I've got some cash around here somewhere."

Not realizing that Ida stole the cash, Cathy suggested, "Maybe you spent it."

"I don't know," he replied as she walked into the room and gave her father a big hug.

"I love you so much Dad."

"Yeah. Yeah. I know," Layne said as he returned the hug.

"I'll see you when I get back."

"Okay."

When Cathy walked outside and up to her car, Sheba ran over to her. Sheba looked at the Chevy Cruz and back to Cathy as she started to whine.

"I know that whine. You want to go for a ride, Sheba. Don't you?" Cathy opened the car door and Sheba jumped in. She made her way across the driver's seat and sat in the passenger's seat so that she had a good view of the road.

"Let me give you some fresh air," Cathy said. She started the car and partially rolled down the passenger window for Sheba. "There we go."

The car backed out of the small parking space and headed down Water Street where it turned left on Northwest Catawba Road. It followed the road south as it changed into East Sand Road.

The section of the road between Our Sunset Place Bed & Breakfast and the Five Bells Inn was Cathy's favorite. It was where the road clung to the side of a limestone cliff on the left and dropped off on the right to the rocky beach below. It also offered a picturesque view across the lake to Port Clinton.

After she picked up her prescription, she returned along the same route. She passed the Five Bells Inn and began hugging the cliff on the right side of the road. She entered the tight curve before Our Sunset Place Bed & Breakfast as Sheba sat alertly next to her.

All of a sudden, a rabbit bolted across the road in front of the car to the underbrush along the edge of the sheer cliff. Sheba reacted quickly. Barking several times, she jumped from her seat into the driver's seat as she tried to go out the half open window to chase the rabbit.

The dog's unexpected leap and sudden weight upon Cathy

caused her to sharply swerve the car to the left. In her panicked reaction, she missed the brake pedal and instead depressed the gas pedal, which resulted in a severe steering overcorrection. The car rocketed like a blur to the edge of the cliff where it crashed through the guardrail. It then pitched over the cliff as it became airborne, flying out beyond the cliff and crashing head-first into the rocks below.

Two hours later, a Catawba police car drove past the three lanes of waiting vehicles at the Catawba ferry dock. The car parked and the chief of police, Ryan Sigler, emerged from the vehicle. He spotted Matt Parker and walked over to him.

"Hello, Matt," the ruggedly-built Sigler said in a somber tone.

"Hi Ryan. What's going on?" he asked, knowing that it wasn't normal for the chief to drive down the hill to the dock.

"Is Zeke here today?"

The laughter from a group of children answered the chief's question.

"Oh yeah. He's entertaining a bunch of kids over there," Parker pointed to the nearby covered waiting area.

"Could you please get him and bring him over to my car?"

A serous look crossed Parker's face. "Is he in trouble?"

"No. He isn't. I need to talk to him, Matt."

"Sure. I'll get him."

Sigler returned to the car while Parker walked over to the shelter.

"Hey, Zeke."

"Yes?" Layne looked up with a twinkle in his eyes and a large smile. He had been enjoying the youngsters' attention.

"Ryan is here. He needs to talk to you right away."

"Why? Did Sheba scare someone?" Layne asked.

"I don't know. He looks real serious."

"Oh, all right," Layne replied. He arose and accompanied Parker to the police car.

"Hello Ryan," Layne said as they approached Sigler who was leaning against the front of the vehicle. "You looking for me?"

"Matt, you better stay a moment," Sigler said when Parker started to walk away.

"Sure."

"What's this all about?" Layne asked, disappointed at the interruption to his fun with the children.

"Zeke," Sigler said solemnly as he placed his arm on Layne's shoulder. "I have some bad news. Really bad news."

"What?"

"It's about Cathy. Her car went over the cliff on Sand Road, just south of Our Sunset Place – about two hours ago."

"Is she okay?" a wide-eyed Layne asked.

"She didn't make it. I am so sorry, Zeke."

"Oh no. Zeke, I'm sorry, too," Parker added. "I'll do whatever you need me to do," he offered.

Layne began to wobble and lost his balance. He began to topple over as shock set in. The two men caught him.

"Come on over to the car and sit," Sigler said. They walked the stunned Layne to the passenger side. Sigler opened the door, and they helped Layne sit down.

A subdued Layne sat quietly with uncried tears welling up within him. The pain was visible on his face.

"There's one more thing, Zeke," Sigler said slowly.

Layne looked up with saddened eyes. He couldn't talk. His emotions were overwhelming.

"Sheba was in the car. I'm sorry Zeke, but she's gone, too,"

Sigler said sadly.

An avalanche of grief cascaded down on Layne as he began to weep. It was like his whole world had been washed away by a freak lake storm. His body shook as a feeling of hopelessness swept over him. A growing pain in his chest brought him back to reality.

"My pills. My pills," he uttered as his heart stressed.

"Where Zeke?" Sigler asked quickly.

"My shirt pocket," Layne wheezed as the pain grew and his chest tightened.

Sigler reached into Layne's pocket and pulled out a small tin case.

"These?"

"Yes. Nitro. I need one," Layne grimaced.

Sigler opened the tin and extracted one of the pills which he handed to Layne. Layne quickly popped it in his mouth and under his tongue so it could dissolve.

"Do you want some water?" Sigler asked.

"Yes," he replied weakly.

"I'll get a bottle," Parker said. He went to the nearby dock building and grabbed a cold bottle out of their fridge. Within two minutes, he was handing an opened bottle to Layne.

"Thanks, Matt." Layne said. He raised the bottle to his lips and took a swig of it. Then he rubbed the cold bottle across his brow.

"Are you okay?" Sigler asked.

"I'm better. Give me a few minutes." He took a couple more sips as he tried to compose himself. "Where is Cathy now?"

"She's at the hospital. They tried to save her, but it was too late," Sigler explained.

Layne nodded. "How about Sheba?"

"She's at the police station. She was gone when they extracted her from the car. They found her on Cathy's lap."

"That's strange. Sheba always rode on the passenger side whether it was Cathy's car or my truck. Ryan, do you know what happened?"

"We're trying to piece it together, Zeke. There was an approaching car that saw her swerve and go over the cliff. They called us. No one knows why she swerved," Sigler explained.

Suddenly Layne looked toward his home. "Has anyone told Michelle yet?" he asked in a worried tone.

"Not that we are aware," Sigler responded.

"I need to get up there and tell her before she hears from someone else," Layne said as he started to stand up.

"Whoa there. I'll drive you up. I don't think you should be walking anywhere right now," Sigler said. He extended his arm to prevent Layne from standing.

"I guess you're right."

"Zeke, I'll let the Markets know and everyone else at the ferry," Parker said. "If there's anything you need, you call me."

Layne nodded.

"You might want to check on him a little later, Matt," Sigler suggested. He shut the car door and walked around.

"I'll do that," Parker responded.

The car backed around and headed up to Layne's home. When it reached the house, Sigler asked, "Would you like me to come in with you?"

Layne shook his head from side to side. "No. I'll do this by myself. We're both going to have a tough evening," Layne said. He slowly eased his frame out of the car.

"Let me know if there is anything I can do. I'll check in on you two later," Sigler advised, before driving away.

Layne walked slowly up the stairs to his home and through the front door.

"Hi Grandpa. I'm late for work," Michelle said as she walked around the kitchen counter.

"You better call off," Layne said.

"Why Grandpa?" Michelle asked, not understanding the strange request. She then saw his face. "What's wrong Grandpa? You look like you just lost your best friend."

Layne looked at her as his eyes brimmed with tears. "I did. I lost two of them."

"Aw Grandpa. You sit here in your chair and tell me about it," she said. She then led Layne across the room to his chair. When he sat, the pent-up tears rolled out like a tidal wave of grief. Layne's body started shaking.

Seeing the deep despair that Layne was in, Michelle felt a knot in her stomach as an uneasy surge of realization crept into her mind. Her mother hadn't returned from the quick trip to the pharmacy. "Where's Mom?"

Layne's body shook harder at the question and Michelle surmised that was the reason for her grandfather's uncharacteristic outburst of emotions. "It's Mom, isn't it? Is something wrong? Is she okay?"

"No, Honey. She's gone, and so is Sheba," he murmured between gasps for air.

"No. That can't be. There's a mistake. She's just delayed. Somebody didn't know what they were talking about," Michelle exclaimed. She abruptly took two steps away and transitioned into denial.

"Come here, Honey," Layne said. He reached out his arms to her.

She walked over to him and allowed him to pull her onto his

lap where he held her tight.

His mouth was next to her ear. "It's true. Ryan Sigler was here and told me that her car went over the cliff past Our Sunset Place. They both died."

"Why Grandpa? Why did they have to die?"

"I don't know princess. I just don't know."

"How did it happen?" she asked. She sobbed uncontrollably.

"They don't know."

"It's not fair. It's not fair," she repeated.

"I know."

"What are we going to do without them?"

"We will stay here and I will take care of you," Layne said. He was trying to calm and reassure her. He didn't mention his apprehension regarding his health and Alzheimer's. He'd work things out. He always did.

"We will get past this although nothing we do will ever replace the love your mother had for both of us," he said in an encouraging tone.

Sobbing, she stood. "I'm going to my room. I want to be alone for a while."

"I understand, Honey," he said. He swiveled his chair around to gaze upon the lake.

Behind his white beard, his mouth fell to a frown. His eyes were devoid of their usual impish sparkle. They were as remote as a far-off land. The cry of the seagulls mixed in with his cry. Briny tears washed down his skin and the cracks in his lips.

For the next hour, Layne sat in his chair in silence, staring blankly at the lake. His solitude was interrupted by a knock on the front door. Slowly he got out of his chair and ambled across the room. When he opened the door, he saw the three owners of the Miller Boat Line – Julene, Billy and Scott Market.

Billy spoke first. "Zeke, we are so sorry about Cathy and Sheba."

"We are, too," the other two offered, upon entering the home.

"We know how much they meant to you," Julene said in consoling Layne. She gave him a huge hug.

"Thank you," Layne said. "You all didn't need to come over."

"It was the right thing to do. You're like family to us," Scott remarked seriously. He clenched an unlit cigar between his lips.

"We're here for you and Michelle," Julene said in a soothing tone.

"Whatever you need, just ask us," Billy offered in a serious, but heartfelt tone.

"Thank you."

"We're serious, Zeke," Billy said firmly.

"I know you are."

"Where's Michelle?" Julene asked.

"In her room. I would just leave her alone. She wants to be by herself. And so do I. We've got some processing to do."

"We understand," Scott said. The three headed for the door.

"I'll be sure to have Matt look in on you," Billy said as they walked out.

"Thank you," Layne said. He turned around and looked again at the lake. Later that night, he sat on the deck as the sun set, playing sad tunes on his harmonica.

CHAPTER 10

The Funeral
Port Clinton

The past four days had been anguishing days for Layne and his granddaughter. They each spent most of the time isolated in their rooms as they privately mourned their loss. Layne didn't even venture out to feed Irish Gin. He was too overwhelmed with despair.

Layne didn't want to be bothered with the number of caring friends who stopped by to console them or drop off a meal. He didn't want to talk to anyone. After the first morning of visitors, he placed a sign on the front door which read, "Do Not Disturb Please!"

Jerry Davenport stopped by after hearing the news and offered to help. At Layne's request, Davenport called the funeral home and made arrangements for them to pick up both bodies and cremate them. He also scheduled the calling hours and gave The Beacon and News-Herald a brief obituary for Cathy and Sheba.

After ignoring the calls from Ida and Blair, Layne finally answered and reluctantly told them when the calling hours would take place. He was irritated that Sigler had called the stepdaughters to let them know that their stepsister had passed away. Layne couldn't wait to give Sigler a piece of his mind. He didn't want those women around him, especially at this trying time. All they would show would be crocodile tears, he thought.

This evening, Layne and Michelle were standing with red eyes in a receiving line at the funeral home. They were in front of a table with two urns which held the cremated remains of Cathy and Sheba. Their pictures were set on the table and throughout the funeral parlor.

Much to their consternation, Ida (aka Siren) and Blair were standing next to them and crying fake tears of grief at the loss of their stepsister and Sheba. Their insincerity was obvious to all who walked through the line to offer their condolences. Their attire reflected their lack of respect as they were dressed in low-cut tops and painted-on jeans.

As mourners passed by, Layne was so happy to see his friend Kim Bartish. The curly-haired woman with mischievous eyes was the general manager at the nearby Holiday Inn Express hotel and had been a longtime friend. She had reserved a room for Layne's stepdaughters during the funeral so they wouldn't have to drive back and forth to Toledo.

"Zeke, I am so sorry," Bartish offered. She threw her arms around him and gave him a kiss on the cheek. She was the queen of compassion. Everyone loved her sweet disposition and quick wit.

"Thank you, Kim. Cathy always treasured your friendship as I do," Layne said. "And thank you for letting the sisters ugly stay there. I didn't want them at my place. No telling what they'd try to steal when my back is turned."

Bartish leaned in and whispered in his ear. "And my even deeper condolences for having them two in your life." She stepped back and they exchanged a grin.

"You always know how to bring a smile to people's faces," Layne said. He watched her hug Michelle and express her sympathy at losing her mother. There was no doubt how sincere Bartish was with Michelle.

Moving down the line, Bartish greeted the two stepdaughters.

"We know you from somewhere," Blair hinted as Bartish stepped in front of her to give her condolences.

"I'm the one who checked you in at the hotel." Bartish wanted to say "Duh," but held back.

Blair squinted down at the name tag that Bartish was wearing. "Oh, of course, how could I forget your name, Kima?" she said as she misread the name.

"It's Kim," Bartish corrected her, thinking what a trip the woman was.

"You should know. It's your name," Blair tried to recover from her gaffe.

"Is your room okay?"

"Yes. Just fine."

Kim stepped away, thinking that she better inventory the room after they checked out to see if anything was missing. She did not like the vibe that she was picking up from the two stepdaughters.

After Jerry Davenport and his wife passed through the line, they sat down in front of two men near the rear of the parlor. They didn't realize that they were sitting in front of Bonehead and Guardrail, who were quietly talking.

"When Siren told me that her stepsister Cathy died, she said we had to go to the funeral. She didn't want to go, but said we all had to go to put on a good show," Bonehead said.

"Yeah, and you had to drag me along," Guardrail complained.

"I wasn't going to come here and end up sitting back here by my lonesome," Bonehead explained. "This really screwed up my weekend."

"Why?"

"Did you forget, stupid?"

"The Blue Bell Run in Detroit?" Guardrail asked.

"Yeah. It's one of the best biker gatherings of the year. Now I'm missing it. How inconsiderate of her to die now! Why couldn't she have just died next week?" he grumbled. "I gotta be here and not in Detroit."

"We could have skipped this and gone there instead," Guardrail countered.

"No. I don't want to cause any friction with Siren. She thinks they're in for a lot of money because of this and I want to be sure I stay tight with her now."

"Smart," Guardrail said.

"For once in your life, you just showed me some intelligence," Bonehead sneered.

Guardrail grinned at the quasi-compliment.

Davenport looked at his wife. "I think I'm ready to go."

"Me, too," she agreed. She rolled her eyes at what they overheard.

As the couple walked out of the funeral home, she asked, "Are you going to warn Zeke?"

"You betcha. It sounds like those two stepdaughters of his are up to no good. He and Michelle need to be alert for anything they try to do."

As the calling hours ended, Blair turned to Layne and advised, "Ida, the boys and I are going out to grab a bite to eat. We'll be over in the morning to see you."

"Okay," Layne said reluctantly. He preferred that they not stop by the next day, but decided to humor them so they'd hit the road and leave him alone.

The funeral home staff had gathered the photos and accompanied Layne and Michelle to his truck. The two of them carried the urns containing the remains of Cathy and Sheba.

"Thank you very much for everything you did for us. All of us," Layne said to the staff. He and Michelle climbed into the truck. He handed Sheba's urn to Michelle and started the engine.

When they arrived home, they carried the urns into the kitchen and set them on the counter.

"I'm going to get changed out of this tie and shirt into something comfier," Layne said. He then headed for his room.

"Me too, Grandpa."

About thirty minutes later, Layne found his way outside onto the deck and dropped into his chair. He picked up Sheba's ball and held it in his hand as he stared at it.

The sun had set and it was a starless sky, even the moon wasn't shining. Only the lights from the Catawba Dock provided any illumination. Can it get any darker? Layne wondered before beginning to weep.

He was lost in a lake filled with hopelessness as waves of grief engulfed him. Like a ship straining to see the light in a storm, he couldn't see what his future was.

Layne didn't hear Michelle walk out the door. She walked over and placed her hand on his shoulder, then bent over to give him a hug.

"I love you, Grandpa," she said softly.

Hiding his depression, he smiled as he reached up and patted her arm. "I know you do, Honey."

"I cried so much I have no tears left," she said grief-stricken.

"That's how I feel too."

"What are we going to do, Grandpa?"

"We'll stay here and I'll take care of you. I'll always take care of you. Cross my heart and hope to die," he said. He then pulled out a handkerchief and wiped the tears from his face. He was worried as to how he could do that as his health deteriorated. There had to be more that he could do, but he'd think it through.

"I really do love you Grandpa. Am I still your princess?"

"You will always be my princess, Honey."

"And you will always be my King!"

"Oh yeah. I'm King of the Lost," Layne joked feebly.

"No you're not. Everyone loves my Grandpa. You will always be my North Star. Guiding me to do the right thing," she proudly declared.

Layne pointed to the dark sky. "There are a couple of new stars up there now. They're real special because they have halos around them. On a clear night, you'll be able to see them and they'll be your mother and Sheba smiling down on us. They're up there with your grandmother. Let's go down to the water's edge."

"Okay," she said as she took his hand and they descended the steps.

Layne reached into his pants pocket and held out his open palm. "I brought you down here because I have a pocket full of stardust."

"Grandpa, that looks like lint to me," Michelle giggled as she extended her hand.

"No Michelle. Close your eyes and feel the magic of the moment." Layne then bent over and grabbed a handful of sand from the beach. He let it fall from his hand through her open fingers.

She giggled again. "Grandpa, you're so special."

"Am I?"

"You are," she said. Hearing thunder and seeing a lightning strike on the horizon, she said, "We better get in before the rain starts."

"You go ahead. I want to stay out here a few more minutes."

"Okay. I'm going to bed. I feel better after our chat and I'm tired," she said. Michelle offered her grandfather one last hug and headed up the steps to go inside.

Layne remained outside as he watched the storm approach from the northwest. With her going inside, he released any pretense of being able to cope with his grief. His body shuddered as he wept. His heart was filled with emptiness. Numbness pounded his brain as he lost control of his body and tumbled to the ground.

As the rain began to pelt down on him, he lay on the sandy beach next to the rocks. The rain turned into a deluge and soaked him. Slowly he stood. He reached into his other pocket and withdrew Sheba's red ball. He looked at it as raindrops washed across his face, mixing with his tears. He cocked his arm back and weakly threw the ball for the last time as far as he could into the water.

Walking as if in a mindless trance, he turned and made his way through the downpour up the steps into the home. He opened the door and walked through the mobile home to go to his bedroom.

Confused, he opened the front door and walked out into the rain. He stood there for a couple of minutes as he tried to remember where his bedroom was situated. The emotional strain was taking its toll on his memory.

He walked back into his home and, confused, opened every door as he walked down the hall to find his bedroom. He was disoriented and afraid at not being able to find the familiar surroundings of his bedroom. Finally, he found it at the end of the hall. Still drenched from the storm, he dropped onto his bed and fell into a tortured sleep.

CHAPTER 11

Layne's Home
The Next Day

It was noon when the door opened suddenly and the dervish devils entered the quiet abode.

"I thought you were going to be here at 10:00," Michelle said as she watched Blair and Ida enter the home.

"We slept in, child. And besides, we don't answer to you or your grandfather," Ida scowled at Michelle. Any pretense of care had completely evaporated.

"Where is the old geezer?" Bonehead asked. He walked inside and was followed closely by Guardrail.

"He's out on the deck," Michelle answered. The others circled her like vultures circling their prey. "He's not doing well."

"What do you mean?" Ida snapped.

"Ever since last night, it's been like he's in a trance. He's just not acting like he's all there."

"That's no surprise," Bonehead chuckled as Guardrail snickered.

Blair looked out on the deck. "Let's go see him," she said to Ida.

"Wait. What are these?" Ida asked as she spotted the two urns from the funeral home.

Before Michelle could respond, Blair interjected, "I think you're the one with Alzheimer's, Ida. That's Cathy and the mutt's ashes."

"I keep telling you to call me Siren," Ida glared at her sister.

"Yeah. Her name's Siren, Blair," Bonehead added.

"Oh whatever. Let's go outside."

The two women paused at the slider door as their faces became pasted over with fake smiles on their cracked lips.

"It's showtime," Ida said.

They went out, leaving Michelle inside with the two bikers.

Bonehead eyed Michelle. "You're looking mighty pretty there, Sweet Britches."

Michelle was repulsed by his unwanted overture. She replied with a death stare.

Bonehead crossed the room in a few steps and abruptly pulled Michelle against him. "When you come and live with us, you and I are going to become real close buddies," he leered.

Twisting away, Michelle wheeled and gave Bonehead a sharp kick in the knee cap. "Not in your lifetime!" she warned. She then strode across the room to the door to the deck.

"Don't be too sure of that Sweet Britches. We all have plans for you and that old coot out there," Bonehead gloated.

"Yeah. They do," Guardrail added with an evil look in his eyes.

Opening the slider and slamming it behind her, Michelle joined the two women on the deck. She wasn't surprised when she saw the two fawning over her grandfather. She was disgusted by their phony display of love for him. Watching them made her feel nauseated.

The deck slider opened and Bonehead stuck his head out. "Hey Siren."

"Yes?" Ida said, while looking at him.

"Guardrail and I are going to head up to that bike rally in Michigan. We can still be a part of it even though we missed yesterday because of that stupid funeral." He virtually spat out the last few words to show his displeasure at having his plans interrupted.

"Go ahead. We'll see you tomorrow at our house," Ida replied.

Bonehead eyeballed Michelle with a wicked smile before he left. Within a couple of minutes, the roar of the two motorcycles in front of the mobile home filled the air and announced their immediate departure.

Blair smiled as she walked over and hugged a reluctant Michelle. "Now it's just us. We're all going to be such a happy family together."

Michelle looked down at her grandfather. His eyes were glassy and he appeared to still be in a trance-like state.

"Has he spoken to you?" Michelle asked.

"No," Blair said. She nodded at Ida with a conspiratorial glance.

"Oh, I need to use your bathroom," Ida said as she went into the home.

For the next fifteen minutes, Blair babbled on with no response from Layne. Michelle was bored and tired with her unconvincing ramblings about what a happy family they would soon become.

The door to the deck slid open and Ida appeared. She wickedly smiled and winked at Blair. "I'm ready to go."

Blair's fake façade crumbled into a grimace. She had no more interest in discussing their future plans. She spoke sharply. "We have to go, but we will be in touch with you two. You can count on it."

Blair followed Ida out to the car. Once they were driving away, she asked, "Did you find it?"

"Yes. But it took me longer than I expected."

"Where was it?"

"In his nightstand drawer."

"Let me see it," Blair grabbed the envelope and withdrew the document. It was Layne's will.

"What does it say? Are we in it? How much do we get?"

"Let me see here," Blair said. She carefully scanned the document. "Here it is. Oh no!" she groaned.

"What? What?"

"We get 10%."

"Each?"

"No. We split it."

"That cheap twit!" Ida roared in disgust. "Who gets the rest?"

"Cathy and in case of her death, it goes to Michelle."

"But she's a minor."

"I know. We'll get that fixed. I know a lawyer in Toledo who owes me a couple of favors. We'll get this all fixed and get us made into Michelle's guardians."

"There's one problem," Ida offered.

"What?"

"He's not dead."

"That won't be a problem. That could work out better for us. We'll get him put away in a nursing home and get the court to appoint us as his guardians. Then we can access his bank account and any savings," Blair explained. She displayed a sinister smirk as her eyes narrowed and she tilted her head to the side.

"That sounds good to me."

"That's why I'm the smarter twin," Blair said coldly.

Ida was still focused on getting her hands on the money and didn't react to the comment. "When do we start?"

"Tonight. I have an idea how this will play out," Blair said with cool detachment.

"I want to know how much he has," Ida said firmly. They pulled into the Holiday Inn Express parking lot and parked. They exited the car and continued talking as they walked toward the lobby.

"A month before Mom died, she told me that he had around $200,000 saved up. I bet it's more now."

"We need to know how much for sure."

"In time we will," Blair said as they entered the lobby. "We need to put him in a nursing home right away."

"Hello ladies," a voice called from the check-in desk.

The two looked to their left and saw Kim Bartish behind the desk.

Blair nodded her head and the two continued plotting as they walked to their room.

After the two left the mobile home, Michelle sighed with relief. "Grandpa, are you okay?"

Layne nodded his head, although his eyes still had that faraway look in them.

"I don't trust them. They're up to no good. And that Bonehead really creeps me out. He's always staring at me and trying to touch me."

Michelle walked around Layne's chair and stood in front of him. "He said that they were going to make me move in with them and he was going to be my close buddy. I don't want that. I don't want anything to do with him. He scares me!"

She slumped against her grandfather and sobbed into his

chest as she clutched his shirt. He rocked her slowly as her tears streamed down her face onto his chest.

"Things will work out."

"I'm scared," she cried. "And you're not yourself either."

"I'm okay. I've just been out of sorts."

"That Bonehead said they have plans for us. What did he mean by that, Grandpa?"

He continued patting her back. "It sounds like they want you to move in with them because they probably don't think I can care for you."

"I don't want to leave you. This is my home. It's with you. You're the only family I have," she moaned.

"Don't you worry, Honey. Nothing is going to happen. Come on now. Let's go inside. I need to get something to eat and then go over and feed Irish Gin," he said. She stepped back and he arose from his chair.

She walked to the door and slid it open. "Oh no!"

"What?"

"The urns are on their side."

"What?" Layne asked again. He followed her into the home and to the kitchen counter.

Michelle picked up her mother's urn and looked inside. It was empty. She checked Sheba's urn and it was empty, too.

"They did something to their remains," Michelle moaned as she turned to her grandfather. She was surprised to see her grandfather standing with a huge smile on his face.

"They may think they did something with the contents, but they didn't. I don't trust them as far as I can spit. I knew they were coming over and set a trap for them. They took the bait."

"What do you mean?"

"The cremated remains were in a plastic bag in each of the

urns. When I got up this morning, I put the two bags in two old coffee cans in my room. Then I took some of the ashes from that little covered grill outside and put them in each urn. Your mother and Sheba are still with us," he assured her.

"Oh Grandpa, you are so smart," she said in a relieved voice. She wrapped her arms around him. "Thank you, Grandpa."

"On some days, my old brain seems to work pretty good. At least it did when I got up, then I had a bit of a relapse."

"How about a peanut butter sandwich?" he offered as he walked behind the counter.

"That sounds tasty."

"I need something tasty, too," he added. "Those two sisters leave an ugly taste in my mouth. Like vomit."

"Ugh. Can we change the topic, Grandpa? That thought isn't appetizing," Michelle asked sweetly.

CHAPTER 12

Barn 4 Horse Corral
Lime Kiln Dock

"Up! Layne commanded to Irish Gin. The horse reared up with her two front legs high in the air.

"That's my girl," Layne said. She settled down on her four legs and nudged Layne's shoulder. "Looking for a carrot?"

The horse whinnied, then snorted, and Layne produced a carrot from the bag at his feet. He had neglected her for the last few days as the turmoil around his daughter's death had distracted him.

Layne turned to Michelle. "Aren't you glad that you came over on the ferry with me?"

"I guess. It's good to be out of the house."

They had caught the late afternoon Miller ferry over to South Bass Island to spend some time with Irish Gin.

"Feel like doing something different?"

"What Grandpa? And if it's riding Irish Gin, the answer is still no."

"Let's go inside the corral."

"Why?"

"So we can give her some attention. I've given you a lot of attention these past few days. It's her turn now," he encouraged his granddaughter.

"I guess."

Layne opened the gate and the two walked inside the corral. Irish Gin trotted over to them and nuzzled Layne's shoulder again. In return, Layne stroked her neck and spoke in a calm voice to her. "That's my girl. You missed us, didn't you?"

Layne looked at Michelle who was standing behind him. "Come on next to me and pet her. She'd love the extra attention."

Michelle reluctantly stepped forward and began stroking her back. When she did, the horse twisted her head and neck away from Layne and began to nuzzle Michelle.

"See. She really likes you."

"I don't think so. She's just looking for a carrot."

"Here then," Layne said. He reached down and gave Michelle one of the carrots.

Michelle held out the carrot and the horse chomped away at it.

"That's a girl. Now you try my trick on her. Go ahead and say it," Layne suggested. He then stepped back.

"Up" Michelle commanded the horse, who reacted by standing on her two rear legs. When she returned to all four legs, she nuzzled Michelle again.

"Have any more carrots, Grandpa?"

"Here's my last one."

While she was feeding it to the horse, his cell phone rang.

"Hello?"

"Zeke?"

He thought about hanging up when he heard the shrill voice. Instead, he answered. "Yes, Blair."

"Ida and I have been talking and we'd like you to come over

to our hotel room to talk with us."

"When?"

"Can you come now?"

"I'm on South Bass Island." He glanced at his watch. "There's a ferry departing in ten minutes. We can be on it."

"We?"

"Michelle and me."

"Okay. We'll be waiting, but don't bring Michelle."

"That's fine," Layne commented. It would be an opportune time for him to tell them they could forget any thought of Michelle moving in with them. "I should be there in about forty-five minutes."

"We will be waiting," Blair said before ending the call.

Layne turned around and saw that Michelle and Irish Gin were getting along well. He hated to pull them apart, but knew he had to.

"Come on Michelle. We have to catch the ferry."

"Is everything okay?"

"Fine. I just had an unexpected meeting come up. I have to be there in about forty-five minutes."

"Okay."

The pair headed for the ferry and return trip back to the mainland. While Michelle ached with profound sadness over her mother's death, she felt so accepted by the demeanor of her horse, Irish Gin. In fact, just being there with Layne and the horse, she felt an overwhelming sense of comfort that momentarily calmed her emotions.

While she could not forget the pain and horror of the accident when her horse threw her off, Michelle allowed that the incident was in the past, as was sadly enough, the recent fatal crash claiming the lives of her mother and the family dog. She realized she could not change any of the past events. Somewhere in her grief and remorse, Michelle believed in Irish Gin and also believed that recent events would not forever define her life in a negative manner.

She vowed, as a 17-year-old girl growing up now with just her ailing grandfather alive, that she would be stronger and more resilient in moving forward. This is what her mother gave her, and Grandpa and Irish Gin too – the will to remain strong and steadfast in the face of adversity.

The two headed for the ferry and took it back to the Catawba Dock. Layne saw Michelle safely inside the mobile home and grabbed his truck keys. "I should be back in a couple of hours," he advised. He then walked out the door.

At the hotel, Ida watched impatiently from the window. "I don't see his truck. Where is he?"

Glancing at her watch, Blair answered, "He should be here any minute."

"Forty-five minutes are up," Ida moaned.

"Maybe he was delayed."

"I don't know."

"When he walks in the room, I want to tell him that I dumped Cathy and Sheba's ashes down the toilet. That should really set him off." Blair's eyes gleamed with cold malice.

"Put him right over the edge! Maybe give him a heart attack," Ida suggested eagerly. "That would solve our problem. He could die in front of us," Ida said as she bristled in anticipation.

"No. We don't want to do that tonight. We just need to get him riled up in front of the police. I want to save telling him about dumping the ashes for when we drop him off at the nursing home tomorrow. Then we will have another incident to show how incompetent he is," Blair declared.

"Whatever you say," Ida said. She then stared out the window like a cobra waiting for its prey. Her narrow eyes seemed like black, inky pools. "He's pulling in now!"

"I'll call him," Blair said as she dialed Layne. "Zeke?"

"Yes?" Layne answered. He parked and turned off the ignition.

"We're on the first floor." She gave him the room number and added, "You will have to pound hard on the door when you get here. I might be in the bathroom and Ida will be taking a shower."

"Okay," Layne said as he hung up.

"Call the police now. Hurry!" Blair ordered Ida, who had slinked across the room to stand next to her sister. She picked up her cell phone and called the police.

"9-1-1. What is your emergency?"

"Yes, we have an emergency," Ida excitedly began. "There's a man trying to break into our hotel room. His name is Zeke Layne. We think he's going to kill us!" she screamed with fake terror.

The dispatcher took the location name and room number. "The chief is nearby. I'll send him right over."

"Hurry!" Ida cried incoherently, before ending the call.

"You should be an actress," Blair said approvingly.

"Let the fun begin."

Ida was filled with eager anticipation as Layne entered the lobby and saw Kim Bartish at the check-in desk.

"Evening, Kim."

"You going to visit your stepdaughters?" she asked. Bartish walked around the counter and gave Layne a bear hug. "Ah, my dear Zeke."

"Yeah. Not what I really want to do. I can think of a lot of better things to do with my time. I rather visit a proctologist than visit with them!"

"They are two weird women," Bartish commented. "I've seen a lot of folks come through here, but those two are certainly different." She released him from her hug and stepped back. "How are you doing? This is the first time I've seen you since the funeral."

"I'm existing if that's what you want to call it."

"How about Michelle?"

"She is in the dumps. What would you expect when you lose your mother and best friend?" He looked down the hall. "I guess I better go see the two masters of disaster."

"I'll see you on the way out," Bartish called.

He ambled down the hall where he calmy approached the women's room and knocked on the door. When there was no response, he knocked harder. Again no one responded. Remembering what Blair had said on the phone, he made a fist and slammed it several times against the door while yelling," Ida! Blair! Let me in!"

The ladies screamed from the other side.

"What are you doing, Zeke?"

Layne turned his head and saw Chief Sigler running toward him. Close on his heels was Kim Bartish.

"I'm trying to get in the room," he retorted angrily. He was becoming confused between the screaming inside the room and the sudden appearance of the police chief.

"Just settle down, Zeke," Sigler said in a stern tone. "Everything's going to be okay."

The ladies continued to scream.

"Ladies, it's okay. The Catawba Police are here now," Sigler shouted.

The two sisters stopped screaming and the door opened slightly.

"Just a moment, ladies," Sigler said. He immediately recognized them as Layne's two stepdaughters. "Zeke, what's going on? Why are you after them?"

Layne had a bewildered look on his face. "What do you mean? They asked me to come over here. They told me to pound on the door."

Sigler looked at the ladies. "Is that true?"

"No, it isn't," Blair stormed. "He turned up here and was threatening us. He was yelling at us and we were scared that he wanted to kill us. Isn't that right, Ida?"

"Yes, he was," Ida replied. She pretended to wipe tears from her eyes. "I was scared."

Sigler turned to Layne. "Zeke, can you tell me what's going on?"

Between the grief and stress of the past few days and this unnerving incident, Layne was emotionally overwhelmed. He leaned against the wall behind him. He felt his life spinning out of control, and he felt a sinking moment of despair as his shoulders slumped. He slid to the floor with a blank stare in his eyes.

"Zeke, are you okay?" Sigler asked. A second police officer then appeared.

Layne didn't respond. He glanced upward with his mouth pursed slightly open. His head was spinning so fast that everything was a blur, but he slowly nodded his head.

Concerned that Layne may be suffering a heart attack, Sigler asked, "Are you having any chest pains, Zeke?"

Layne shook his head negatively.

Not wanting to take a chance, Sigler radioed in for the rescue squad.

"I have a pass key. We can take him in the room next door and lay him on the bed," Bartish suggested.

"That's a great idea," Sigler said. He motioned to the other officer to help him get Layne to his feet.

Bartish opened the door to the room and the two police officers half-carried Layne to the bed.

"I'll go to the lobby and wait for the squad," Bartish said. She disappeared down the hall.

Sigler left the other officer with Layne and walked across the hall to the two sisters' room. They were standing on the other side of the room when he entered.

"You say that Zeke threatened you?" Sigler asked.

"Yes," Blair answered.

"What exactly did he say?"

"Open the door or I'll kill you both."

"Yeah. That's right," Ida chipped in.

"Why would he say that?" Sigler asked.

"I don't know. I think he's really losing it. I think the strain of everything is taking a toll on his mental health," Blair commented.

"Yeah. I do, too," Ida echoed like a parrot.

"That's really strange. I've known Zeke for years and I've never heard him threaten harm to anyone."

"He did to us. He's going downhill. He needs to be placed in a home!" Blair said sternly.

"Or he's going to kill someone," Ida babbled mindlessly.

"Do you want to file a complaint?" Sigler asked, weary of talking to the two women who seemed to be on a mission.

Blair feigned a look of concern. "Oh no. We don't want any harm to come to our dear stepfather. We are just concerned about his well-being."

"Yeah. And he'd be better off in a nursing home," Ida jab-bered.

Blair shot Ida a look that said for her to shut up, then turned back to Sigler with a false sense of heartfelt emotion. "We want the best for him."

Sigler frowned. He recalled past discussions with Layne about the ill intentions of his stepdaughters. He wasn't buying in on their counterfeit display of concern.

"The squad's here," Bartish said from the doorway as two paramedics entered the room across the hall and began to check Layne's vitals.

"I'll be right there," Sigler said before turning back to the two stepsisters. "Thank you for your time. I'll write this up as we normally do."

"Thank you," Blair said.

Sigler looked at Ida who had turned on the TV and fo-cused her attention on a cartoon. Very concerned, indeed, Sigler thought to himself as he left the room.

Within ten minutes, the paramedics were wheeling Layne down the hall for a run to the hospital to have him checked out.

"Let me have your keys, Zeke," Bartish said as he went by. "We'll get your truck back home for you."

"Thank you, Kim. I'll be fine," Layne mumbled from the gurney.

Bartish and Sigler followed them to the lobby where the two stopped to talk.

"Something fishy is going on here, Ryan," Bartish began.

"Why do you say that?"

"When Zeke arrived, he stopped for a moment to say hello to me. He wasn't in any hurry and wasn't upset about anything.

In fact, he was quite calm."

Sigler took a deep breath. "Based on what I heard from those two stepdaughters, I'd say the only people in a hurry here tonight are those two. And I'd guess they want to hurry Layne into a nursing home."

"That wouldn't surprise me."

"They actually mentioned it a couple of times."

"Does Zeke know?" Bartish asked.

"I don't think so."

Two hours later, Layne's cardiologist walked into Layne's hospital room.

Layne looked up at him and smiled. "Did you get the test results?"

"Yes, and they looked fine," Dr. Schaffner answered. "You didn't have a heart attack, although we still need to do that surgery that you keep putting off. It would help your quality of life."

"No. No. I don't want any surgery John," Layne countered. "What caused my little episode back there?"

"Probably stress overload," Schaffner guessed. "How are you coping with your grief?"

"It's tough, but I'm working my way through it."

"You need to take it easy."

"I've been taking it easy ever since I retired."

"I've talked with D'Arcy and we both have a concern about the growing issues with your sporadic memory losses and their increasing frequency."

"Oh, I'll be okay," Layne pooh-poohed their concern. "Can I go home or do I have to spend the night?"

"You can go home."

"Are my conniving stepdaughters out in the lobby?"

"I didn't see them."

"I can see they're real concerned about my health," he said sarcastically.

"Can I have the nurse call anyone for you or get you a cab?"

"What time is it?"

"Almost ten."

Layne laughed. "I'll call Jerry Davenport and get him out of bed."

Within thirty minutes, Layne was riding in Davenport's Jeep.

"Which way are we headed to my place?" Layne asked as they pulled out of the hospital parking lot.

"Up Sand Road."

"Can we go the other way? Up Route 53? I don't want to drive by the place where Cathy and Sheba died. I'm not ready for that."

"We can do that. I understand."

As Davenport drove, Layne relayed the evening's events to the best of his ability.

"Those two are a real piece of work," Davenport sighed.

"I'm not going to let them win!" Layne said with a determined look on his face.

"I know you won't. Whatever you need, Zeke, I'm there for you and Michelle."

"Thanks Jerry. You've always been a good friend."

"I'm serious. When do they leave town?"

"If they had their way, it would be over my dead body," Layne shot. "And with my savings in their pocket," he added.

"Leeches, huh?"

"I bet if you looked that word up in the dictionary, you'd find their names listed," Layne suggested.

When they arrived at the mobile home, Layne stepped out of the Jeep and started to cross the road.

"Hey Zeke! Where are you going?"

"Home," Layne replied as he pointed at the Catawba Inn.

Davenport sighed as he stepped out of the Jeep and walked over to Layne. It looked like Layne was having another memory lapse. He put his arm around his friend's shoulder and turned him around.

"Let me walk you inside so I know that you're okay."

"Sure. Sure. That's fine," Layne said with a confused look on his face.

Davenport walked his friend up the front steps and opened the door. They walked in and were greeted by Michelle.

"Grandpa, is everything okay?" Where's your truck? I didn't hear it drive up." She looked from Layne to Davenport and back.

"He's fine. Let me walk him to his room and get him settled. Then we can talk," said Davenport.

"Okay," Michelle responded.

Ten minutes later, Davenport returned to the kitchen.

"What happened? Did he have an accident?" She didn't want to think about losing him, too.

"No." Davenport relayed the evening events based on what Layne had told him on the ride home. "I think he will be okay in the morning, but you need to keep a close watch on him. If you see that he's not acting normal, give me a call."

"I'm not sure what normal is anymore," she replied. "For either of us," she added.

"You both have been through a lot," he said as he gave her a hug. "I'll give you a call in the morning to check in on you."

As he turned to leave, Michelle asked, "What about his

truck?"

"He said that Kim Bartish will be bringing it over in the morning."

"I'll keep an eye out for her although I'll hear that noisy muffler when she pulls in," she laughed softly. "Thank you, Jerry, for all of your help."

"Any time," he said as he closed the door behind him.

CHAPTER 13

Layne's Home
The Next Morning

The truck's noisy muffler announced its return home. Bartish parked it and exited the truck. She motioned to the driver of the hotel van that had followed her to pull to the side of the road.

"I need to run in and return the keys. I'll just be a sec," she called to the van driver, Martha. She then went up the steps and knocked on the door.

"Come in," Layne responded.

Bartish entered and saw Layne sitting in his easy chair. He looked a lot better than the previous night. "You're looking good."

When he started to get out of the chair, she urged, "Don't get up because I'm here. You just relax. I'll put your keys right here on the kitchen counter."

"Thank you, Kim."

"No problem. Did your stepdaughters follow you to the hospital?"

"No shows."

"That doesn't surprise me. They seemed to be all giggly when they walked through the lobby. They must have gone out to celebrate because they were feeling no pain when they returned and headed to their room."

"They don't have any of the Layne blood flowing through their veins," Layne grumbled thankfully.

"I'll say. I don't know if they have any kindness in them anywhere, based on what I've seen."

"I know what you mean."

"They seem like real drama queens."

"Trauma queens would be more like it," Layne suggested wryly.

Kim chuckled. She then remarked, "I need to get back to the hotel." She walked to his chair and gave him a hug. "My dear, sweet friend."

"Thank you again for your help."

Halfway to the front door, Bartish stopped and looked back at Layne. "Zeke, there's something I should tell you."

"What's that?"

"I'd be careful with those two and I know I'm not telling you anything you don't already know. Ryan said they have plans to put you in a nursing home."

Layne nodded his head. "Doesn't surprise me one bit. I'll be careful."

Bartish walked out, pulling the door closed.

A few minutes later, Michelle walked down the hall. "Good morning, Grandpa. Are you feeling better?"

"Yes, I am."

"What do you have planned for today?"

"I'm thinking I might head over to the dock and entertain some of the kids. What do you want to do?"

Before she could answer, the sound of car doors slamming signaled the arrival of visitors.

"Take a peek out the window and tell me who that is," Layne urged his granddaughter.

She walked over and looked out. When she turned to face Layne, she displayed a huge frown.

"It's Blair and Ida."

"The human versions of a walking migraine headache," Layne cracked. Michelle retreated to the kitchen. He now was on his game.

The door opened and Heckle and Jeckle burst into the trailer.

"You're still with us, Zeke?" Ida inquired.

She was answered by a loud noise. She narrowed her eyes as she glared at Layne. "Did you just fart?"

"No. My butt just blew you a kiss."

Ida wrinkled her nose in disgust as Blair piped up. "You must be feeling better."

"Better than your best day on earth," Layne cracked.

"What did they tell you at the hospital?" Ida asked.

"I'm as fit as a fiddle."

Layne then smiled like a Cheshire cat to their consternation. He wasn't going to share anything about his heart condition with those two vultures. They were probably circling his bank branch in eager anticipation.

Blair spotted his truck keys on the counter and walked over. "I'm going to take these," she said. She then quickly snatched them like a pit viper attacking its prey. "We don't want to take any chances of you driving that truck in your current mental state."

"Yeah. We don't want to risk you losing your life. We love you so much," Ida cooed as she feigned concern.

It didn't work on Layne. He knew better.

"Hi Michelle. I didn't see you standing there," Blair said as Michelle glared at her.

"Hello," Michelle replied slowly, not wanting to engage in any conversation with either of the trolls.

"Did you grandfather tell you what happened to him last night? About going to the hospital and all?" Blair asked.

"Yes."

"We need to take really good care of him," Ida added.

"Then can you get me a long hose?" Layne interrupted.

"A hose?" Ida replied. "What for? What do you need a long hose for, old man?"

"One end I'll hold to my nose. The other end you connect to the tail pipe of my truck. Then, start the truck. I'll be just fine."

"Grandpa!" Michelle shrieked.

"I knew it. He's off his rocker Blair. His wants to commit suicide!" a wide-eyed Ida squealed.

"Michelle, you just heard what your grandfather said. You're a witness. He's suicidal!" Blair added.

"He was just kidding. He wouldn't do anything like that, right Grandpa?"

"I need to step outside and make a phone call," Blair said. She walked over to the door, slyly winking at Ida.

Taking her cue, Ida turned to Layne. "Why don't you and me go outside and take in the beautiful view of the lake?" she asked in a syrupy tone. It was disgusting.

"We can do that."

Layne was somewhat surprised and wondering what they were up to. He arose to his feet and the two walked out the slider to the deck.

In front of the home, Blair was talking on her cell phone. "We should be there in an hour. He doesn't know what we're doing, so you may find him a bit resistant when we arrive. We'll have to bring his clothes and personal items over tomorrow."

Two minutes later, Ida walked out the front door and joined Blair as she finished her phone call.

"Was that the nursing home?" she asked eagerly.

"Yes," Blair said as she slid her cell phone into her jeans pocket.

"Is everything set?"

"Yes. It won't be long now. We'll have completed the first part of my plan," Blair said with an air of confidence.

"I can't wait until we get to the money part of the plan," Ida gleefully offered.

"We'll go through this place with a fine-tooth comb tomorrow when we come back to get that little brat, Michelle."

The slider slid open and Michelle rushed out on the deck to join her grandfather. "Grandpa, I was spying on Blair and Ida."

"You were?"

"They're going to trick you."

"How's that?" he asked.

"They're going to take you to a nursing home and leave you there today."

"That's their plan, huh? Probably one close to them in Toledo."

"Then they're coming back tomorrow to get me and take me to live with them. I don't want to live with them and I don't want you to go to a nursing home. I want us to live together," she said in a worried tone, almost in tears.

There followed several moments of eerie silence. Michelle began to sob gently as her sadness deepened. Layne wrinkled his brow as he tried to think with some degree of clarity. "I need my memory not to fail me," he willed himself.

"Don't you worry, Honey. I'll somehow work this out for both of us," Layne forcefully declared.

"Oh Grandpa, you're the best," Michelle said. She hugged him and put all of her trust in him.

"Just play along with anything I do and don't worry. Okay?"

"Okay."

"Just stay calm."

The door to the slider opened and the two sisters walked out onto the deck.

Blair spoke first. "Zeke, things got blown a little out of proportion last night and we'd like to make it up to you."

"You would?"

"Yes," Ida butted in. "We're going to take you for ice cream."

"You are?"

"We have a special place on the other side of Port Clinton that we want to take you to," Blair suggested.

"That's sounds mighty nice of you. Can Michelle come to?"

"No. We want it to be a special time just with you," Blair explained.

"Yeah. A special time with you," Ida added a little too eagerly.

"We'll take her another time," Blair added as she squinted at Michelle.

"Okay then," Layne said as he stood from his chair and adjusted his thick- framed glasses. "I need to get my cap."

The four of them walked inside. As Layne neared the kitchen counter, he moaned and grasped his chest, then suddenly collapsed to the floor.

"My chest," he groaned.

Ida's eyes bulged. "He's having a heart attack. Call 911

Blair."

Blair looked at a worrying Michelle, wishing she wasn't there because she'd just let him lie there and die. Reluctantly, she pulled out her cell phone and called 911.

Michelle knelt on the floor next to Layne. "Grandpa, can I get you anything?" she asked. She momentarily forgot about their recent conversation on the deck.

"No. I need to get to the hospital," Layne groaned. He glanced at the two sisters to be sure they weren't watching. He then winked at Michelle and gave her a quick smile before starting to moan again.

Michelle nodded as she realized that this was part of his improvised ruse. She relaxed, but kept up the worried front for the benefit of the two sisters.

Within ten minutes, the rescue squad arrived, and the paramedics checked Layne's vitals.

"How is he doing?" Blair asked.

"It's looking okay now, but we're going to run him to the hospital."

The squad brought in a gurney and placed Layne on it. They took him outside and put him in the back of the ambulance. Two minutes later, they were racing to the hospital.

Blair turned to Michelle. "Ida and I are going to the hospital to make sure he's okay. You just stay here and we'll let you know."

"Okay."

As the two sisters drove away, Michelle worried how their appearance at the hospital would impact Layne's plan, whatever it was. She occupied herself by cleaning up the deck and kitchen area.

"We're going to the hospital?" Ida asked as they drove.

"No. If he survives, they'll probably keep him overnight for observation. Then we'll pick him up tomorrow and take him to the nursing home. It will just push everything back one day."

"That sounds good."

"Hopefully, he dies. That would just make dealing with everything so much easier," Blair said. Her evil mind calculated possible outcomes.

CHAPTER 14

Layne's Room
The Hospital

The hospital room was stuffy and the air had a hint of bleach to it. The walls were painted a light yellow and featured a couple of illustrative lake view art prints. Overhead the ceiling was made from polystyrene squares laid on a grid-like frame. A bright overhead light highlighted the cracks in the slate gray tile floor.

Layne stared around his room from his uncomfortable bed as his mind raced. He wasn't surprised by the results of the tests. Of course, he knew that he hadn't suffered a heart attack. He had used the entire time from the ambulance ride through the tests to being wheeled into his room to plan. Little did the staff know that he had no plans on staying through the next morning for observation.

He reached for his cell phone and called Jerry Davenport.

"Hello Zeke. How are you doing today?"

"Fine Jerry, but I need your help big time."

"Sure. Anything. I'm here for you, my friend."

"I'm in the hospital. Nothing to be worried about, but I need to bust this joint. Can you come over and pick me up?"

"Are you sure that you're okay?"

"I am." Layne relayed a quick summary of what had happened that morning to the best of his ability.

"Oh no. What a mess!" Davenport said in awe. "Are your stepdaughters still at your place?"

"I don't know. If they are, they are probably stealing Cathy's jewels. Next thing I know, they'll be after my jewels."

Davenport chuckled softly. He knew his aged pal all too well.

"Jerry, I've been laying here thinking."

"That sounds dangerous," Davenport teased.

"I've made some serious decisions and I'll tell you more when you pick me up."

"I'll be right over."

"Before you come, I need you to pull a favor with your cousin at AAA."

"Sure. What is it?"

Layne outlined his plan and Davenport agreed to do his part. They ended their call and Layne called Michelle.

"Grandpa. Where are you?"

"I'm at the hospital."

"You're okay, right? You were just faking it, right?"

"I'm fine. Just fine. Are you ready to mess up the twin schemers?"

"I am, Grandpa," she said firmly. "What are we going to do?"

"We're going on the run. It'll be an adventure for you and me," he said confidently.

"What? What do you mean? Where are we going?"

"I'm going to borrow Jerry's horse trailer. Then we're going to load up Irish Gin and head down to see your cousin Donna on Chincoteague Island."

"That's where grandma is buried, right?"

"Yes. And that's where Irish Gin is from. We'll take your mother's ashes and Sheba's with us so we can bury them next to your grandmother."

"How long are we going to be gone?"

"I don't know, but you'll get to skip the start of school," he added. He didn't know what they would end up doing long term. It was all he could do to plan this trip.

Michelle was a bit hesitant about leaving the area where her friends were, but she knew that the two sisters were going to force her to leave anyway – and she didn't want to be around that Bonehead character.

"Okay. What do I need to do?"

"Pack only what you need. I want to be on the road in an hour or so. I'm pretty sure that Blair and Ida are on their way back to Toledo. I'll look for their car when we drive by the Holiday Inn Express," Layne instructed.

"They haven't been back here since they left after the ambulance. They told me they were going to the hospital."

"No shows. You just can't believe a word they say. Now, you go and get ready. I'll be there shortly."

"Wait. How are you going to drive your truck? They took your truck key and the spare key that was hanging on the cabinet."

Layne smiled. "I have another spare key that I keep in my wallet in case I'm out and lose my other key." He didn't tell her that he also kept a round for his pistol in his wallet, too.

"Now girl, you go get ready."

"Okay." She hung up and ran down the hall to pack.

Layne swung his body around in the bed so that his legs were over the side. Before he stood, he decided that he better say a quick prayer. He bowed his head and prayed, "It's going to be a busy day, Lord, and I need your help and a clear mind. If I forget you during the day, please don't forget me."

Fifteen minutes later, Layne had changed into his street clothes and was standing in front of the lobby when Davenport arrived.

"That was quick," Layne said as he climbed into the Jeep.

"I dropped everything to help you. We're not going to let those sisters hijack your life," Davenport said. They departed the hospital grounds and drove off. Glancing at Layne, Davenport added, "You look really good. Probably the best that I've seen you look in a long time."

Layne beamed. "I'm energized. I'm getting out of Dodge while the getting is good. I need to stop at the bank, too. Got to get some cash."

They stopped at the AAA office and picked up the Trip-Tiks that Davenport had requested. They stopped at the bank where Layne withdrew cash from his savings account. When they pulled out of the bank parking lot and drove slowly past the Holiday Inn Express, Layne eyed its parking lot.

"I don't see their car. They must be gone."

Davenport turned left on NW Catawba Road and they followed it to East Barnum Road where they turned left. Davenport backed up to the side of his sign shop where the horse trailer was parked. The two men exited the Jeep.

"I cleaned out the trailer as best as I could, Zeke," Davenport's wife offered. She walked around the trailer to greet them.

"Looks like that right tire needs some air. Let me get my mini-compressor," Davenport advised as he walked away.

"I really appreciate your help, folks."

Layne indeed was very appreciative of the assistance provided by the Davenports. He walked around the tandem-wheeled trailer to inspect it. It looked like it hadn't been used in years. He was unsure of its roadworthiness, but didn't have a choice.

The top third of the horse trailer was a faded light green giving way to a rusty brown. It had been a two-horse trailer originally, but later converted to a one-horse trailer. The Dutch doors were open at the back, and Layne saw that the old plank floor had a rubber mat on top of it.

"You'll want to spread some wood shavings on the floor," Cathy Davenport said. "We don't have any, otherwise I'd put some there for you."

"I can get some at the barn before we load up Irish Gin."

"Jerry bought this to haul our granddaughter's horse and he hasn't had a chance to rehab it. You know how he's good at those types of things," Cathy explained.

"He's amazing. That boy has some talent. I don't know how in the world he comes up with all of the different designs for his sign work," Layne replied.

"Just a dash of luck mixed with hard work," Davenport said. He walked around the corner and began to inflate the tire.

"Zeke, the brake lights work fine, but the right turn signal light has a short in it and doesn't work all the time," Davenport cautioned.

"I'll make do. I used to work with a guy like that."

"How's that?" Davenport asked, a bit confused.

"He had a short in him and didn't work all the time," Layne chuckled. He felt good. His mind was clear and sharp.

"I'm impressed how well your memory has been so far today," Davenport countered.

"I'm on a mission. Focused. Very focused," Layne said with strong determination.

A couple of minutes later, they were hitching the trailer to the back of the Jeep and heading to Layne's place.

When they arrived, Davenport parked the trailer in front of the mobile home. "I'll give you a hand in hitching it to your truck," he offered.

"Thanks, Jerry."

Layne pulled the hidden key out of his wallet and walked over to his truck.

They spent the next ten minutes jockeying the vehicles around and unhitching and hitching the trailer. When they were done, Davenport shook hands with Layne.

"You be careful, my friend, and take your time. There's no rush in getting where you're going or returning the trailer."

"You've always been there to help me when I need it," Layne said appreciatively.

"And to let you win at euchre," Davenport teased.

"I win fair and square."

Davenport glanced at his watch. "You better finish up here so you can start your drive."

"You're right," Layne said. He observed Michelle standing on the small front porch where she watched them hook up the horse trailer. "Thanks again, Jerry." Layne said as he headed for the front steps.

Davenport opened the door to his Jeep and saw that Layne had left the AAA TripTik. He grabbed it and ran after Layne. "Zeke, you forgot this," he said. He handed the bag containing the TripTik to Layne.

"I'm doing pretty good if that's all I forget today," Layne grinned. He took the bag with a certain air of confidence in himself.

"Drive safely," Davenport said. He returned to his Jeep and

drove away.

Layne walked into the mobile home with Michelle. "Are you finished packing?" he asked. He pulled out the TripTik from the bag and tossed the empty bag into the trash can.

"Pretty much. And Grandpa? Don't forget your meds."

"There are days when I'd like to," he mumbled. He walked over to his closet and pulled out an old worn suitcase. He placed it on his bed and opened it. He then opened the nightstand drawer and picked up his Smith & Wesson. Placing it on top of the nightstand, he reached into his wallet and withdrew the lone bullet, which he then loaded into the revolver. "Just a little insurance," he thought to himself as he set it next to the suitcase.

Layne quickly packed and placed the revolver on top of his clothes, then closed the suitcase. He picked up the coffee cans containing Cathy and Sheba's ashes and headed back down the hallway.

He saw that Michelle was making sandwiches and had prepared a cooler filled with beverages. "Somebody's thinking ahead," he said proudly.

She smiled. "I've got my part to do, too, Grandpa."

"Be sure you pack whatever carrots we have for Irish Gin."

"Already in the cooler."

Layne walked out of the house and placed his suitcase in the back of the pickup. He opened the door of the truck and placed the coffee cans in the middle of the bench seat. After he closed the door, he leaned against the side of the truck and made a phone call to call in a favor. He explained what he needed and ended the call.

Walking back inside the mobile home, he asked, "Are you about ready, Michelle?"

"Yes. Can you carry my suitcase and backpack out to the truck?"

"I can do that."

"Be careful. I have my laptop in the backpack."

"I'll be careful." He carried them out to the truck.

When Michelle walked out of the mobile home, she stopped and stared at the rusty horse trailer. "You're going to put Irish Gin in that wreck?" she exclaimed in disbelief.

"It'll be fine. Just wait and see," he said as he took the cooler of food from her and placed it in the truck bed. He then pulled a worn tarp over it and their suitcases.

"I don't know, Grandpa." She shook her head from side to side as he entered the truck. "Grandpa!"

"What?"

"Look. I can see the ground when I look down through the floor of your truck."

"That's not a problem as long as it doesn't rain or we drive through a puddle. You might get some water splashed up at you," he grinned. "If it bothers you, I can throw a blanket on the floor so you won't see the holes."

With a wary look, Michelle said, "Let's give it a try. You think we can make it in this truck?"

"Sure we can. She burns some oil, but I've got a gallon of oil in the back. I'll check it every morning and add it if I need to."

Michelle picked up a small rectangular device that was on the front seat. She examined it and turned to her grandfather. "What's this?"

"That, my dear, is a stud finder. That's what you grandmother used to find me," he grinned. He then started the truck.

Five minutes later, they were in line with other vehicles, waiting to drive aboard the Miller Ferry.

"What're you up to with that raggedy-looking horse trailer?" Parker asked as he approached Layne's truck.

"Matthew, don't tell anyone if they come asking, but we're taking Irish Gin back to Chincoteague."

"In these vehicles?" Parker asked skeptically. He eyed the worn pickup truck and the dilapidated trailer.

"We'll be fine," Layne assured Parker. "And if we have a mechanical problem, I can handle most things."

Parker saw that the line of vehicles had started moving.

"You better get going then. You drive safely." He looked at Michelle. "You take good care of your grandfather."

"Oh, I will."

She smiled at Parker, then dwelled upon the thought that she, in fact, was Layne's only caregiver.

They drove aboard the ferry. During the twenty-minute ride over to South Bass Island, Layne called Billy Market to tell him that he was picking up Irish Gin. He was glad to hear that Market's wife, Allie, and their son Liam, were at the corral as they would be able to help load up Irish Gin.

When the ferry arrived at Lime Kiln dock, the vehicles drove off the ferry and up the steep hill. Layne's truck and trailer turned right as they exited and drove over to the corral at Barn 4. After they parked, Layne and Michelle walked to the rear of the trailer and opened the Dutch doors.

"Hi Zeke," a cheery voice called.

Layne and Michelle turned around and saw the youthful-looking blonde, Allie Market, approaching them. She was one of the island's favorite entertainers. She also was an experienced and knowledgeable equine handler and rider who often would visit Irish Gin.

They exchanged greetings and Allie expressed her condolences to them as Liam joined the group.

"Where are you going with that trailer?" Liam asked.

"We're taking Irish Gin back to her home," Layne replied to the boy.

"In that?"

"Liam, you're sounding like me," Michelle laughed softly.

"Exactly what I was thinking," Allie added.

"We'll make it," Layne assured them.

Allie looked into the rear of the trailer. "I've got an extra water and feed bucket you can have, Zeke."

"That would be a big help. You have any wood shavings for the floor?"

"We do and I've got hay and extra feed you can have."

For the next twenty minutes they loaded shavings into the trailer and spread them before affixing two buckets to hooks by the hay manger in the trailer. They added hay to the manger and stored some extra hay and feed above and below the manger. Allie also gave them extra wood shavings to use after they mucked out the trailer each day.

"I've another manure and bedding fork you can have to clean out the trailer," Allie said as she handed it to Michelle. "I guess you'll be doing all the cleaning, Michelle."

"Oh yeah. I don't think Grandpa wants to do any of that."

"I've been dealing with a lot of manure these past few days. I don't need any more," Layne cracked.

Michelle stowed the fork and turned to Layne. "Should you get Irish Gin now?"

"Sounds good to me. Do you want to lead her to the trailer and into it?"

Michelle wasted no time in replying. "No. You can do that." Michelle was still skittish about being around the horse.

"Are you sure?"

"Absolutely," she said firmly.

"You get your tack and store it in the trailer. I'll bring Irish Gin out."

Layne approached Irish Gin. "How are you doing, girl?" he asked as he gently stroked her head.

She nuzzled against him, looking for a carrot.

"I know what you want," he said. He stepped away and attached a lead to her halter. "Come along with me and I'll get you one in a minute."

Obediently, she followed him out as he led her into the trailer. After he fastened his end of the lead to a hook inside, he began walking to the rear.

"I heard you, Grandpa," Michelle said. She handed him a carrot. "I got it out of the cooler for you."

"Thank you."

Layne then walked back to Irish Gin. "Here you go, girl," he said. He then extended it to her and she began to gobble it up.

Layne returned to the back of the trailer and shut the two bottom doors. Turning to face Liam, Allie and Michelle, he asked, "What am I forgetting?"

"I'd say you have everything under control," Allie said, "except for goodbye hugs."

"I was just coming to that."

"How long are you going to be gone?" Allie asked as she gently embraced Layne.

"Probably a couple of weeks at least. I've got to sort some things out. Like I said, there's been a lot happening in the last few days."

"I'll say," Michelle added.

Layne and Michelle got in the truck and waved goodbye as they headed for the return line for the ferry.

Thirty minutes later, they were back on the mainland and driving off the ferry at the Catawba Dock.

"Where to now? Grandpa?"

Layne picked up the AAA TripTik that he had studied on the ferry ride and handed it to Michelle. "You're going to be my navigator on the trip. This tick-tock will tell us what roads to go down."

"I can do that!" she said proudly. She took it and glanced at it. "Grandpa, it's called a TripTik, not tick-tock," she chuckled.

"Whatever. The first part should be easy. It takes us to Norwalk to pick up Route 18 to the outskirts of Akron. I've got to stop there and see a friend. Then it takes us by New Philadelphia and Cambridge. It'll be getting late then and we'll find ourselves a hotel."

Two hours later after driving at a leisurely pace, Michelle directed him to turn off Route 18 and had him drive to Embassy Parkway.

Michelle looked from the TripTik to the addresses in front of a number of office buildings.

"There it is. Turn here, Grandpa," she pointed to a building on the right.

He turned right into the parking lot of a large three-story office building and drove to the back where there was ample room to park the truck and trailer.

"I'm going inside to take care of some business. You stay here and mind the truck and Irish Gin. Maybe you can give her a carrot."

"Okay. What do you have to do here?"

"Just meet with some people. It's all good," he assured her

as he stepped out of the truck.

Thirty minutes later, Layne walked out of the building. He smiled when he saw Michelle engaging with Irish Gin. "You two are getting to be real good friends on this trip."

"Maybe," she said as she walked back from the trailer and jumped into the truck.

Layne pulled back the tarp in the bed, opened his suitcase and placed a large envelope inside. He then closed the suitcase and pulled the tarp back over everything before getting back into the driver's seat.

"It's almost five o'clock. We may hit some rush hour traffic when we drive through Akron and Canton," Layne advised.

"You can do it," Michelle encouraged as she focused on the map that would take them to Interstate Route 77 South.

Layne smiled as he started the truck and drove them out of the parking lot.

They did catch rush hour traffic from Akron to Canton. Layne added to the traffic congestion a bit as he drove along at ten miles below the posted speed limit. Nearby drivers were increasingly frustrated and blasting their horns as they passed him.

Layne ignored them even though Michelle implored him to speed up.

"Grandpa, you can go faster!"

"We're doing just fine. I don't want to push this truck or trailer. This truck hasn't gone this far in years," Layne commented cautiously. "And neither have I."

Two hours later, they pulled into a low, one-story motel in Cambridge. It definitely had seen better days. The weatherworn sign in front read "Sunrise Motel."

"You stay here and I'll go see if they have a room for us and if they don't mind allowing Irish Gin to stretch her legs."

"Okay Grandpa."

Layne got out of the truck and almost fell. He grabbed the door handle to keep his balance.

"Are you okay Grandpa?"

"Just a bit tired. Got to get my sea legs back," he responded weakly. Layne was surprised at how tired he was.

"You want me to walk with you?"

"No. No. I'm fine."

When he returned, he walked slowly. In his hand, he dangled a room key.

"We are all set. Turns out they are horse lovers. They gave us the room at the very end and said we could park over there," he said as he climbed into the truck and started it.

"What about walking Irish Gin?"

"They said no problem. They said we could muck out the trailer and leave the manure. They'd use it for their garden."

"Come on. Let's see what our room looks like," he said. He parked, then exited his truck.

They walked to the room and he unlocked the door. He swung open the door and saw a sparse room. The two twin beds were covered with thin quilts. There was a chair, small dresser and an old TV set.

"Looks perfect," he said. He ignored the look of disdain on Michelle's face. "I've got to use the bathroom. Why don't you bring in your suitcase?"

Michelle returned to the truck and retrieved her suitcase and backpack. She took them into the room and saw that the bathroom door was still closed. She decided to bring in her grandfather's suitcase and the cooler.

When she returned, she found her grandfather laying atop

one of the beds, asleep and gently snoring. He was fully clothed and still wearing his glasses. She reached over and gently took them off his head before placing them on the nightstand.

She pulled off his shoes and partially covered him with a blanket as his snores filled the room. She realized that the poor guy was tired out from his long day and she'd have to take care of Irish Gin. She wasn't excited about it, but she couldn't leave the horse unattended.

It had been a long time since she interacted with her horse and mucked out a stall. She was very leery as she approached the trailer. In her hand, she held a carrot. She opened the Dutch doors and stared inside as she fought to overcome her fear of being near the horse.

"Irish Gin, it's me, Michelle," she said softly. The horse gently swung her head around to look at Michelle. She softly whinnied when she spotted the carrot in her hand.

Michelle stood frozen. Her heart was pounding. It was pounding so hard that she thought it would rupture through her chest. She looked around to see if anyone was near enough to hear it beating.

She tried to slow her breathing in an attempt to calm herself as a cold sweat covered her. She gripped the hard metal door with one hand for security.

"I've got this. I can do this," she said quietly to encourage herself.

Timidly she placed one foot in the trailer as she kept a close eye on the horse's rear flank. "I'm going to take care of you so don't you kick me," she begged. She gently placed a hand on Irish Gin's rear flank and allowed it to follow along her back and to the withers as she carefully slid along the wall to the front of the trailer. "That's a good girl."

Michelle felt a growing confidence. "Here's your carrot," she said as she held it out to Irish Gin. As the horse began chomping it down, Michelle reached around and untied the lead rope. She then began moving carefully to the rear of the trailer as she held the lead rope. "Come on girl. Let's stretch your legs," she murmured, then clicked her tongue.

The horse turned and followed her out of the trailer and to a grassy spot under a tree where Michelle tied the lead.

"You stay here and enjoy the grass," she said. She returned to the trailer to muck out the manure and replace the wood shavings. She also filled the feed and water bucket and added more hay to the manger.

When she was done, she leaned against the trailer's door and wiped the sweat from her brow. She was pleased with the job she had done. She spent another thirty minutes watching the horse graze as the sun set on the horizon.

Michelle then walked over to the tree and untied the lead. "We're going back inside the trailer now. Come on, girl," she urged the horse as she clicked her tongue several times. Michelle wasn't as nervous this time as she led the horse back to the trailer. Her confidence indeed had returned.

"Thank you, girl. Bless you."

After she secured the lead to the manger, she surprised herself as she stroked the horse's head a couple of time. "You're such a good girl." She then walked out of the trailer, closed the doors and returned to the motel room.

Earlier in the day, Blair called the hospital in Port Clinton to check on Layne's condition. She was hoping that he had passed away and was stunned to learn that he had disappeared.

"This is good, Blair," Ida smiled wickedly. "He's probably wandering around town. He doesn't know where he is."

"I'm surprised to hear myself say this Ida, but you're right. It's just another reason why he needs to be in a nursing home."

"Yeah and maybe they'll find him dead!"

"That would solve all of our problems."

"Are we going to drive over there?"

"No. We just drove back to Toledo. I don't want to make another drive there this afternoon. We'll go tomorrow and pick up Michelle. We'll get Bonehead and Guardrail to go with us. We might need their muscle to throw Layne in the car and take him to the nursing home."

"Yeah. That's a good idea, Blair."

CHAPTER 15

Layne's Home
The Next Day

"Why did we have to leave so early, Blair?" Ida moaned as they approached Layne's place in Blair's car.

"If he's here, we'll catch them off guard by getting here early."

"And the hospital still can't find Zeke!" Ida retorted.

"That's what they said when I called this morning. They've got the police and community out looking for him. But he could have caught a ride home."

Her car was followed by Bonehead and Guardrail on their Harleys as it rounded the curve and then approached Layne's mobile home.

"I don't like what I see," Blair said. She quickly wheeled into the parking space next to the mobile home.

Ida looked around. "What? What? I don't see anything."

"That's the problem, dummy. Where's Zeke's truck?"

Ida's eyes bulged. "It's gone! Maybe Michelle took it."

"Don't you remember anything. She didn't know how to drive a stick shift. She told us that on one of our visits."

"Oh. I guess you're right."

"Of course, I'm right. Besides, I have both truck keys here in my purse. I wonder how someone drove it away."

"Maybe it was towed," Ida suggested.

"I doubt it. I've got the house key on the chain. Let's go inside."

The two women exited the car as the two bikers parked next to them.

"Blair, I think it would be a good idea for me to take Michelle back to Toledo on my bike," Bonehead suggested. "We can tie her on behind me if we need to." Bonehead was anxious to get up close to Michelle. "That will make it easier for you with Zeke in the car. You'll just have one to manage."

"We'll see," Blair offered. She inserted the key in the front door. She swung open the door and they all walked in.

"Michelle! Michelle! Are you home?" Blair called out. She walked down the hallway to the bedroom. She peaked inside and saw it was empty.

"I think she's gone," Ida called from the bathroom. "Looks like her hair brush and makeup are missing. I checked the medicine cabinet and all of Zeke's medicine is missing, too."

"Good detective work," Blair said. They met in the living room. "That means that someone found Zeke. I wonder what they're up to."

"This could be a clue," Bonehead suggested as he saw the AAA bag sticking out of the wastebasket. He picked it up and read the side of the bag. "Zeke Layne. Catawba to Chincoteague."

"That's where they got that horse for Michelle," Blair exclaimed. She reached for her cell phone.

"What are you going to do?" Ida asked perplexed.

"Watch and learn." She searched the web for the Port Clinton AAA office phone number and dialed it. "My stepfather misplaced the TripTik you gave him. Can I come down right away to pick up another?" She paused. "Yes. It's for Zeke Layne."

Blair was smiling like the cat that ate the canary. "He stopped by and picked up one yesterday around noon. They will have another one ready in a bit."

Ida heard the comment and walked out of the mobile home.

Bonehead looked at Guardrail. "Ready for a little game of chase?" he asked with a malicious grin.

Guardrail nodded his head.

"What do you mean?" Blair asked.

"We'll ride down and pick up that TripTik and see what roads they are taking. In that old rickety truck of his, he can't be too far ahead of us. We'll chase him down and bring them both back."

"That's a great idea," Blair said.

"We can hog-tie them and throw them in the back of the truck if we have to," Bonehead added.

Just then, Ida walked back inside. "I'm the real detective here," she proudly exclaimed.

"What do you mean?" Blair asked.

"I went over to the ticket booth and told them we were trying to find Zeke. The lady there told me that she saw him and Michelle leave yesterday in his truck and he was pulling an old rusty horse trailer." Ida was beaming.

"This is your day, Ida," Blair commented at hearing the news.

"That should make it easier to catch up to him. He'd be going even slower if he's pulling a horse trailer," Bonehead surmised.

Blair nodded.

"I guess Guardrail and I will head over to the AAA office and pick up that TripTik, then we'll go after them."

"Good. It's around the corner from that Holiday Inn Express we stayed at," Blair advised.

"Let's hit the road," Bonehead directed. He walked out the door with Guardrail following him. Within a minute, the sound of their roaring bike engines signaled their departure.

"What are we going to do?" Ida asked.

"Since no one is here, we're going through this house with a fine-tooth comb. Let's see if we can find his financial records and anything of value," Blair suggested. She headed for Layne's bedroom.

Meanwhile at the Sunrise Motel in Cambridge, Michelle was trying to wake her grandfather.

"Grandpa, wake up. You've been sleeping for more than twelve hours," she said. She gently shook him.

"I'm tired, Michelle. Let me sleep a little longer," he moaned. He was drained from the events of the prior day. "My brain is on five percent battery," he announced in a low voice. He then turned over in total exhaustion. He was so drained that his bones were tired.

Deciding to let him sleep longer, Michelle took the room key and went outside to check on Irish Gin.

"Are you okay, girl?" she asked. The horse gazed at her from the open trailer window, then neighed in response.

"How would you like to stretch your legs?"

Michelle walked around the rear of the trailer and opened the doors. She confidently walked inside and led the horse out. She then led her around the grounds for twenty minutes before returning her to the trailer. All the while, Michelle continued to worry about her grandfather's condition.

Michelle wandered down to the motel office to see if they offered a continental breakfast. She opened the door and saw a room to the side that had a couple of tables. There was a counter along one wall that had a Keurig coffee machine and a box of cereal. Next to the cereal was a pitcher of milk.

Slim pickings, she thought as she helped herself to a bowl of cereal. After she poured milk into it, she picked a table in front of a large window that overlooked a stream running through a stand of trees. When she finished eating, she poured a plastic cup full of milk and filled a bowl with cereal for her grandfather. She set them on a tray she found and made a coffee for him.

When she returned to the room, she set the tray of food on the dresser and sat on the edge of her grandfather's bed.

"Grandpa, you've got to get up. Like you used to say, we're burning daylight."

Layne moaned as he rolled over. "Okay. I'll try."

Michelle stood and extended her hand. "Let me help you sit up."

Layne took her hand and moved to a sitting position with his legs hanging over the edge of the bed. His vision was clouded with a hazy fuzz. He tried to focus as he looked around the room.

"Where are we Michelle? This doesn't look like my bedroom," he said, somewhat confused.

"We're in a motel room," she answered with a worried look on her face. "In Cambridge, Ohio."

"Great googly moogly. What are we doing in a motel room?" Layne asked in bewilderment.

"Grandpa, we're on our way to Chincoteague. Don't you remember?"

Michelle believed that Layne was having one of his episodes.

"No. I don't." Layne tried hard to remember, but his mind was skipping a beat. Spotting the food, he suggested, "Maybe I'll remember after I eat."

"Here's your glasses. I cleaned them. They were so dirty I don't know how you could see through them."

"I do just fine with them. My, you sound just like your mother!"

Michelle reached for the tray of food and set it on the bed next to him. "I'll pour your milk on your cereal," she offered. She remained very concerned about his state of mind and overall physical well-being.

He was bleary-eyed and munching slowly on his cereal. Suddenly, he stopped munching. His jaw went slack. Milk dribbled out of his mouth. His eyes glazed over blankly.

"Grandpa, are you okay?" Michelle asked in a soothing voice even though she was scared out of her wits. She wondered if the stress of the prior day triggered a hit to his memory bank.

"I'll be fine. I'm just a bit out of sorts," he said as his eyes seemed to return to normal. He rubbed his unwashed beard and commented, "I need to shower. Can you help me up? I'm just a little weak this morning."

"Sure Grandpa."

Michelle became somewhat relieved to see the sparkle begin to reappear in Layne's eyes. She helped him to his feet, but her confidence about his state of mind and overall health remained unsettled.

"I'll be fine. I'm just tuckered out from yesterday. It took a bigger hit on me than I expected." He opened his suitcase and grabbed a change of clothes.

"I won't be long," he said as he closed the bathroom door behind him.

Michelle turned on the TV and waited patiently for Layne to finish. She kept an ear cocked to the bathroom in case he needed assistance.

Twenty minutes later, the door opened and he rambled into the room.

"Grandpa! What am I going to do with you?"

"What do you mean?"

"Your zipper is down!"

"Oops," Layne said as he quickly reached down and zipped up.

"And your shirt buttons are buttoned in the wrong hole," she giggled.

"I did that?" Layne asked with a smile. He was returning to his old self which was a relief to Michelle.

For the next few minutes, the two of them packed up. When Michelle was distracted, Layne took his .38 caliber handgun out of his suitcase and put it in his pocket.

"Ready to go?"

"I am, and I gave Irish Gin a walk this morning," she said proudly.

"That's a girl. You're getting more comfortable with her," Layne said, pleased at her initiative. "You go ahead and stow our gear in the back of the truck. I'm going to wander back and say good morning to Irish Gin."

"Okay. I've got this," Michelle said as he walked out of the room.

When Michelle left the room, she spotted her grandfather standing next to the road in front of the motel. "Grandpa, what are you doing?"

"I'm flagging down a cab," he answered, mildly irritated that she didn't see that he was helping them get a good start for the day.

"Why?"

"To take us to our next stop."

"But we're driving Grandpa!" She pointed to the truck and trailer. "That's your truck."

Layne looked at the truck and trailer and a look of realization crossed his face. "Oh yeah. I remember now." He headed for the trailer.

When Layne reached the rear of the trailer, he swung open the door and reached inside to a small compartment on the wall. He opened it and pulled the .38 out of his pocket. He placed it inside the compartment and swung the door shut. Then he stepped up to the front of the trailer and spent some time with Irish Gin.

"All set, Grandpa," Michelle called from the rear of the truck. She again was greatly worried about his state of mind. Her hope was that his Alzheimer's symptoms might subside as the day wore on.

"Okay, I'll be right there," Layne said. He exited the trailer, then closed the bottom half of the Dutch doors behind him. "I better check the engine oil, too."

Layne lifted the hood and checked. "We're down about a quart. I'll add some."

He grabbed the gallon container of oil and added some to the engine before again checking its level with the dipstick. He added a bit more and rechecked.

"There we go, all set now."

"Grandpa, would you like me to drive? I have my temps."

"I didn't think you knew how to drive a stick shift."

"I don't, but I'm a quick learner."

Layne looked back at the trailer. "I don't think now is a

good time to learn. We've got that trailer back there. That complicates driving."

Based on what she experienced with his driving the day before, he was the one who complicated driving, she thought quietly. She walked to the truck and took her seat.

Layne shut the hood and returned the container to the truck bed. When he eased himself into the driver's seat, he looked at Michelle. "We're going to get some gas over there," he said, pointing to a gas station next to the motel. "I believe then we'll be ready to hit the road."

"Okay. You sure do look a lot better than when you woke up," Michelle observed with relief. She now could see his clarity of thought perhaps returning for the remainder of the day.

"I feel much better. I guess yesterday took way more out of me than I expected."

Two hours later, they were driving along the Interstate Route 470 bypass around downtown Wheeling, West Virginia.

"This is a big bridge, Grandpa," Michelle said as they drove over the river.

"That's the Ohio River below us and I've got something I need to do here. It's on my bucket list."

"What's that, Grandpa?"

"I'm taking a dip in the Ohio River," he declared as he took the first exit and drove down to the wooded river bank. "You can take Irish Gin out and let her stretch her legs while I take a swim."

"What about the current? Aren't you worried about that?"

"I'm just going for a quick dip, child. It's not like I'm swimming across the river," Layne scoffed at her apparent concern.

"Okay, and you better be careful."

Layne found a spot on the side of the road where he pulled

over and parked. "I'm going on the other side of those trees," he said.

"Okay."

Michelle went to the rear of the trailer and led the horse out while her grandfather grabbed a towel out of his suitcase. She made a mental note of where he entered the woods so that she could check on him.

Fifteen minutes later, she was leading Irish Gin down to the river to get a drink of river water. What she saw would scar her memory for years.

"Grandpa!" she exclaimed. She observed her grandfather standing naked with his backside toward her. He was dripping wet. "Where are your clothes?"

"I can't find them," he said without turning around. "The current took me down river a bit and I don't remember where I went in."

"You stay right there and I'll find your clothes," she said. She tied the horse's lead rope to a nearby tree and went off in search for his clothes. "And don't turn around Grandpa!"

"I wasn't going to."

It only took her a few minutes to find them strewn on some rocks. She picked them up and took them back to him.

"I'm going to set them here for you. Give me a minute to get Irish Gin and lead her away. We'll meet you back at the truck."

"I always wanted to go skinny-dipping in the Ohio River," Layne said to himself, proud of his accomplishment.

When he heard their footsteps moving away, he turned and began putting his clothes on, then headed back to the truck.

"See. That wasn't so bad."

"Maybe not for you, but I didn't need to see your scrawny, naked butt," she called out from inside the trailer. She finished securing the horse for the next portion of the drive. When she emerged, she added, "And neither did Irish Gin. I'm going to give her a carrot to help get over her trauma."

Layne laughed as he got into the truck and she withdrew a carrot from the cooler. After she fed it to the horse, she climbed back in the truck and they headed to the I-470 bypass.

Shortly after the bypass merged once again with Interstate Route 70 east of Wheeling and started going up a huge hill, they encountered a problem. The truck engine died.

"What's wrong, Grandpa?"

"I'm not sure," he said as the vehicle came to a stop along the highway shoulder. He then carefully opened the door as traffic flew up the hill and walked around to the front and opened the hood. After inspecting the engine, he declared, "I think it's the fuel pump."

"I'm going to need a new one." He walked over to the passenger side of the truck. "Do you think you can use that smart phone of yours and find out where the closest auto parts store is?"

"Sure," she said. She reached into her backpack and withdrew her iPhone. In less than a minute, she called out, "I found one. It's about two miles behind us. I have it on a map."

"Let me see," Layne said. He peered at the display screen through the open window.

"Yep. I can go there and get a new one."

"You're going to walk back there?"

"No way, girl. Irish Gin is going to take me there," he smiled.

"What?"

"Come on and help me get her out of the trailer and saddled up. Good thing we brought your tack with us."

"I'll say," she chuckled softly. She thought about the sight of her grandfather on the horse.

They opened the Dutch doors and led the horse out to the side of the road next to the guardrail, where the ground dropped away sharply to a rock-filled valley.

"I'll hold the reins and you put the blanket and saddle on her. You won't need to adjust the stirrups seeing as how we're both about the same height," Layne instructed.

Michelle bent to her task and had the horse ready to ride after a few minutes.

"You better be real careful riding her with all of this traffic whizzing by," Michelle cautioned.

"That won't be a problem. We'll cross over to the median strip and ride in the grass," he countered. "Empty the feed bucket into the feed bin and bring it out to me."

"Why?"

"So I can step on it to get my foot into the stirrup. I'm not as spry as I once was," he explained.

"Okay." She went inside the trailer and did as he requested. When she returned, she placed the feed bucket upside down below the stirrup.

"Now, you're probably going to have to give me a lift up."

"I can do that," she assured him.

"I know you're a strong girl so don't heave me up and over the other side," he joked as he placed one foot on the bucket and one hand on her shoulder to steady himself.

"I won't."

"Okay. Let's do it. Heave ho," Layne directed. They worked together to sit him in the saddle. He landed where he wanted to be and secured his feet in the stirrups. "Hand me the reins and I'll be good to go."

"Here you go, Grandpa."

"You keep your cell phone handy. I have mine with me," he instructed before he started out.

"One thing, Grandpa," Michelle mentioned.

"What?"

"Don't forget where I am. You couldn't remember where your clothes were when we were at the river, remember?"

"I'll remember. You're a lot more important than a pile of clothes," he asserted.

"I hope," she said. She then watched him turn the horse in the direction of the interstate highway median and auto parts store.

"I hope I remember, too," Layne thought. Don't fail me now memory. A break in the traffic allowed him to trot the horse across the three lanes of eastbound highway. Making it safely into the median, he began their trip to the auto parts store.

Forty minutes later, two bikers went through the curve before the straight run up the highway. A fiendish smile crossed Bonehead's face when he recognized the truck sitting on the side of the road ahead of them. He caught Guardrail's attention and pointed to it. Guardrail, in turn, nodded his head in acknowledgement.

When the two bikers neared the old truck and trailer, they pulled up behind it and switched off their engines.

"Well, what have we here?" Bonehead asked with an evil glint in his eye as he looked at Michelle sitting nearby on the guardrail.

Michelle was aghast as she recognized the two approaching riders. She carefully watched but was frozen in the moment as they dismounted and began to approach. Her anxiety surged so fast that she felt that she was going to vomit. As fear replaced it, she then felt her throat thickening and beads of sweat forming on her brow.

"Hey there, Cupcake," Bonehead leered. He carefully surveyed the scene around him. Seeing the open hood of the truck, he sneered, "Broken down? No grandpa around? Just you and me?"

He quickly closed the gap between them and grabbed both of her wrists. Sticking out his tongue, he lewdly licked the side of her cheek as she pulled back in revulsion. "You taste delicious," he said. He then stepped back to ogle her.

"You leave me alone!" Michelle screamed. She tried to twist away from his iron-like grip.

"Oh no, Cupcake. I think you and I are going to have a little fun," he smirked. He began dragging her to the rear of the open trailer.

"My grandpa will be back soon and you're going to be in big trouble."

"Bonehead, you better lay off her," Guardrail cautioned.

"You can have a turn when I'm finished."

Shaking his head negatively, Guardrail said firmly, "This isn't what I signed up for. I'm out of here." He then turned and walked back to his bike.

"You don't know what you're missing," Bonehead snarled at his friend. The bike engine roared to life and Guardrail rode away.

"Now it's just you and me, Cupcake. I've been waiting a while for a taste of you," he hissed. Bonehead threw her to the floor of the trailer and the two began wrestling.

"Keep your meat hooks off my granddaughter! Let her go," a voice shouted angrily from above Bonehead. The biker turned around and began laughing when he saw Layne astride the heavily breathing horse.

"What do we have here? The Grandpa Ranger? Where's your faithful Indian companion, Tonto?" Bonehead jeered. He failed to notice that while he was distracted, Michelle had squirmed out of the trailer and was standing next to it.

"I'll show you what you have here," Layne replied with a determined look in his eyes. He slid off the horse and handed the bag with the new fuel pump and the reins to Michelle.

"Yippee-ki-yay! This is going to be too easy. Bring it on old man," Bonehead sniggered as he faced Layne.

Layne approached Bonehead unsteadily, then suddenly dove for the trailer. Confused by the move, Bonehead swung his body around and saw Layne opening a small compartment on the side of the trailer. When he saw the door swing open and its contents, he pulled back Layne's outstretched arm and grabbed the .38.

"This is your equalizer?" Bonehead scoffed. He looked over the weapon. "It only has one round in it," he jeered with a disparaging look. He emptied the round into his hand and pitched it over the guardrail.

"Mighty nice of you to give me something to use on you. When was the last time you were pistol-whipped?" He had a face with narrowed eyes, filled with malice as he advanced toward Layne.

Layne reached down and grabbed a handful of horse dung and threw it at Bonehead's face in an act of defiance.

Wiping off the pieces that stuck to his face, an enraged Bonehead took a step toward Layne. That's when Michelle stepped into the fray as she brought Irish Gin closer to the rear of the trailer.

"Up!" Michelle commanded. Irish Gin reared back on her two back legs, startling Bonehead.

Without thinking, the biker reacted by quickly taking several steps backwards into the highway – right into the path of a passing semi-truck. His body made a sickening thud as the truck struck it and carried it ninety feet up the road where it crumpled to the side in a bloody pile.

The horse brought her front feet back on the ground as Michelle knelt next to her grandfather. "Are you okay?" she asked. She was in shock at what just transpired.

Layne was feeling pretty proud of his young granddaughter. "Yes. I'm fine. I'm just fine," he gasped. He picked up his glasses, which had been knocked off his head. "Can you get me a water?" He had an ashen gray countenance.

"Sure."

While she was gone, Layne slowly reached into his pocket and withdrew the tin of nitro pills. He popped one under his tongue and waited for the pain in his chest to subside.

When she returned, his breathing had normalized. He took the water bottle and drank. He then looked at her and extended his hand. "Now please help me to my feet."

After he stood, he brushed himself off and looked with deep admiration at Michelle. "That was some quick-thinking young lady. I am so proud of you."

"I was just trying to get him away from you. I didn't mean for him to get hit by a truck. I wouldn't do anything like that." She buried her head into her grandfather's shoulder and her body shuddered at the thought of having caused a man's death. She sobbed almost uncontrollably.

"That's okay. Everything will be fine," Layne said as he comforted her.

"You folks okay?" the truck driver asked. He had pulled over as soon as he could and radioed the state troopers. He then checked the body and saw that Bonehead clearly was dead before proceeding toward the horse trailer.

"I'm really sorry about hitting him. It happened so fast I couldn't do anything," the shaken truck driver explained.

"You did us a favor." Layne went on to detail what happened.

A state trooper pulled off the road and parked by Bonehead's bike. He got out of his vehicle and walked over to the horse trailer. Another state trooper drove by slowly and parked his vehicle near Bonehead's body and checked it. Seeing that he was dead, he called for an ambulance, then walked back to the rear of the horse trailer.

The first state trooper took notes as Layne, Michelle and the trucker explained what had transpired. He took Layne and the trucker's driver's license and went back to his car to run them. While he did, the second trooper called for a tow truck to come and pick up Bonehead's bike.

While they were waiting, Layne stroked Irish Gin's nose. "You saved our lives today, girl. Michelle, why don't you get two carrots out of the cooler for her?"

"Did you gallop the whole way back?" she asked.

"No. Just the last two hundred yards when I saw his buddy ride away on his bike and you there with that shidiot."

When Michelle handed a carrot to Layne, he was surprised to see her keep the other.

"What are you doing?"

"I'll feed her this one."

The second trooper noticed the truck's hood up. "Engine trouble?"

"Fuel pump. I just bought a new one and returned as the ruckus started."

"You didn't get a chance to replace that fuel pump, did you?"

"Not with the unpleasant interruption we had," Layne answered.

"I'll give you a hand," the trooper offered as he placed his hat on the front seat of the truck. "You have any tools?"

"In the bed."

"I'll give you a hand, too," the trucker said as the two men started to work on replacing the pump.

Within a matter of minutes, the trooper asked Layne to try to start the engine. Layne made his way to the truck and stepped inside. He depressed the accelerator a few times and turned the key. The engine started on the second try. He gunned it a couple of times. "I think we're good to go."

While the men were working on the truck, a still stunned Michelle removed the tack from Irish Gin and led her back inside the trailer. She then closed the bottom half of the Dutch doors before walking up to the truck cab. She saw two paramedics wheel Bonehead's body to their ambulance, which they had parked behind the second state trooper's vehicle.

The first trooper joined everyone and returned their drivers' licenses. "Everything checked out. You folks are free to go."

Layne thanked the officers and the trucker as Michelle entered the truck and the trooper retrieved his hat. "We'll be heading out," he said as one of the troopers stepped into the nearest lane and waved traffic into the middle lane to make it easier for Layne to pull out.

Layne tooted the truck horn as they drove away.

The sun streamed through the truck windows, but Michelle's mind was clouded with gray. Her face had a grimace and was contorted with a painful expression as she kept hearing over and over in her mind that sound of Bonehead's body connecting with the front end of the semi-truck.

Layne glanced at her as they headed for Morgantown, West Virginia, where he'd stop for gas. He knew that she was suffering. He sensed it filling the truck cab like a fog of despair.

"I'm sorry that you had to experience that," Layne consoled her.

"I am too."

"What goes around, comes around. Bad things happen to bad people," Layne stoically suggested.

"And good people," Michelle added as she thought about her mother's recent death.

"I guess you're right, smarty!"

Finally, Michelle released her emotions and allowed the pent-up tears to stream down her face. She cried for a while as she blankly stared out the passenger window.

They drove in silence for almost two hours to a gas station in Morgantown where he refueled. They used the restrooms and freshened Irish Gin's water before Michelle took a sandwich out of the cooler for Layne to eat. She didn't take one since she had lost her appetite.

Within twenty minutes, they were back on Interstate Route 68, driving eastward through the Appalachian Mountains to Cumberland and down to Hagerstown, Maryland where they'd spend the night.

"That tick tock said we're going to be driving through the mountains. It should be real pretty," Layne suggested. They continued their drive up the slope near Cooper's Rock State Forest, which was 2,400 feet above sea level.

As they drove, Michelle began to return to the real world. She had to. Layne had driven off the highway onto the berm several times as his attention strayed. It was getting late in the day and Michelle was noting a pattern in her grandfather. He seemed to have focus or memory problems in the early morning and the evening. He was much better during the middle of the day.

A little over two hours later, they pulled off the highway in Hagerstown.

"This old truck of mine is holding up," Layne said. He then smiled as they turned into the parking lot of a motel close to the highway.

"I was holding my breath," Michelle responded. "You were going so slow that those big semi-trucks were passing you – and that was going uphill."

"You noticed, huh? I didn't want to push it," he said as he turned off the engine. "I'll see if they have a room and will work with us as far as Irish Gin goes."

In a few minutes, he was back with a room key. "They said we can take Irish Gin for a walk as long as we were willing to take the room at the far end. And I got a great rate," he said proudly. "When she asked if I wanted the senior discount, I told her I usually get a senile discount."

Michelle laughed. "Grandpa, you are so funny!"

Layne nodded his head as he climbed back in the truck and drove to the last unit. He parked in front and walked over to the room. Unlocking the door, he swung it open and looked inside.

"Looks clean to me," he said. He turned around and headed for the truck. "I'll bring in the suitcases and the cooler. Why don't you take care of Irish Gin?"

"Okay," she answered as she headed to the trailer. On the way, she stopped at the cooler and grabbed two carrots from the cooler. When she opened the rear of the trailer, she stepped inside, patting Irish Gin as she walked to the front of the trailer. "You're such a good girl."

The horse neighed in response.

"Sounds like you two are enjoying each other's company," Layne called. He then lifted the suitcases out of the truck.

"We've become best buddies."

Michelle gave the horse one of the carrots. Untying the lead rope, she had the horse follow her out of the trailer. Her confidence had been restored as far as handling Irish Gin.

"You did so good today, saving us from that bad man," she said. The horse gently nuzzled her shoulder. "Here you go. One more carrot and I'm giving you extra feed tonight as a treat. You and I have become good buddies, haven't we?"

Michelle tied the horse to a nearby tree and began cleaning out the manure and replacing it with fresh wood chips. She added feed to the bucket and again provided fresh water for the horse. After she filled the manger with hay, she returned to the horse's side and stroked her neck as Irish Gin grazed in the grassy area.

After thirty minutes, she returned the horse to the trailer and headed back to the motel room. When she opened the door, she found her grandfather asleep on the bed closest to the window. He was fully clothed and held a half-eaten sandwich from the cooler in his hand.

She took the sandwich and placed it in the cooler. She also slipped off his glasses and cap, placing them on the chair between the beds. After she ate a half sandwich and cleaned up in the bathroom, Michelle laid on the bed. She tried to sleep, but the events of the day were replaying in her mind, especially Bonehead's death. She began sobbing again.

Her cries woke up Layne who looked over at her. "Are you

okay, Honey?" he asked.

"I can't sleep. I've got a terrible headache."

"Come over here."

Michelle rolled out of the bed and stepped over to Layne's bed. She sat down on the edge.

"Where does it hurt?"

Michelle pointed to a spot on her forehead. "Here."

"Bend your head down here," he said. She leaned forward and Layne kissed her forehead. "Is that better?"

"No. You missed it. Over to the side a little."

Layne kissed the spot she referred to.

"Now, is that better?"

"No. You missed it again."

Layne chuckled. "Are you teasing me, you rascal?"

"Yes," she giggled as she began to feel better. She laid on the bed next to him and wrapped her arms around Layne. "I love you so much, Grandpa."

Layne smiled. "I love you, too, Honey."

"I'm glad that we got to take this trip together. I really am."

"A lot better than what Blair and Ida had in store for us," Layne remarked.

"Way better." She didn't say anything for a minute and then asked, "What are we going to do after we take Irish Gin to Chincoteague?"

"I don't know. I've got to sort that out. What do you want to do?"

"I'm not sure other than I don't want to be anywhere near Blair and Ida."

"Neither do I," Layne agreed.

"I miss Mom so much." Michelle said sadly.

"I do, too."

They laid there for a few minutes without talking. Layne fought to keep awake, but a veil of tiredness covered him. He began to snore.

When Michelle heard him snoring, she eased herself out of the bed and returned to her bed. Still fully-clothed, she stretched out on it and finally fell into a fitful sleep.

CHAPTER 16

The Motel Room
Hagerstown, Maryland

The next morning was very nearly a repeat of the prior morning. Layne slept in late and Michelle had a hard time waking him up. He wasn't asleep, she thought. He was in deep hibernation. She realized that the stress of the prior day probably had taken a toll on him and that's why he was so exhausted. His face looked peaceful, almost lifeless.

Giving up, she went outside and took care of Irish Gin. The horse was well-mannered and in good spirits. Michelle's comfort zone around the horse grew with each passing day and chore. She began now to think more of Irish Gin as truly her horse again, and that she was its principal caregiver. Like her grandpa, the horse too, needed Michelle. The young girl felt a new level of maturity emerging within her.

When she returned to the motel room, she found Layne still asleep. "Grandpa, wake up. You've been sleeping for twelve hours again."

Layne slowly pulled the blanket over his head to hide in a cocoon of peace. "A little longer, Michelle. Just a little longer," he softly called out. He quickly fell asleep. He wanted more time to recharge his weary body and especially his mind.

"Okay," Michelle offered. She quietly packed her suitcase and took it out to the truck. She then went up to the motel office to get a couple of containers of ice for the cooler. When she was done, she returned to her grandfather's bedside.

"Grandpa, are you ready to get up?"

He snorted once and then pulled the blanket down from his eyes. As he peaked out, he asked, "Michelle, is that you?"

"Yes," she said, somewhat relieved that his mental state seemed better than the previous morning. "Are you ready to get up?"

"Yes." He stuck out an arm and said, "Please help me sit up."

She reached down and assisted him in getting to a sitting position with his feet on the floor. "Just give me a minute," he said. He then looked around the room, trying to remember where they were. "Where are we?"

"We're in a motel room. We're on our way to Chincoteague. Do you remember?" she asked pensively.

"I remember," he said as her explanation reminded him.

"Okay. You sit there. I'm going to the bathroom real quick. Then I'll help you to your feet."

Layne groggily nodded his head as she walked into the bathroom, closing the door behind her. Five minutes later, she emerged from the bathroom to find Layne had disappeared. The room door was wide open. She glanced upon the dresser and saw that the room keys were still there. She ran out the doorway to look for her grandfather.

"Grandpa! Grandpa!" Michelle called out. She went first to the truck and trailer, but didn't see him. She then looked around the parking lot and ran to the street to see if he had wandered out there, but to no avail. She ran around the back of the motel and subsequently spotted him walking into a wooded area.

"Grandpa! Where are you going?" she called out. She rushed to his side and put her arm around him in an affectionate embrace.

"That Sheba," Layne stammered. "She ran off again. I bet she's chasing a rabbit. She's going to make us late to hit the road today."

Michelle examined her grandfather's face. His eyes had a distant look and his lips were drooping. "Are you okay?" she asked with concern.

"I would be if Sheba hadn't run off like that. I don't know how she got out of the room. She was sleeping next to my bed." The old man frowned and began to wave his arms in the air above his head. He was disgusted. "That darn dog."

Michelle reached up and took hold of his right hand. In a soothing tone, she suggested, "Let's go back to the room and maybe when you finish getting ready, Sheba will be back."

"Okay." Layne looked around. He was lost. He didn't know where he was. He forgot the moment and had no idea what day it was, or the time of day. "I'll let you lead the way, Honey", he offered. Layne was unwilling to admit his mental dilemma or to tell her that he was having some shortness of breath. "Great googly moogly!"

Michelle knew her grandpa was again stricken by his condition.

"Right this way," she said. She gently walked him back to the room. When they arrived, Michelle looked him over. He seemed to be a little more alert, but she was uncertain. "How do you feel now, Grandpa?"

"I'm fine. Let me go and get cleaned up," Layne responded. He walked to his suitcase to grab a fresh change of clothes.

"Why don't you see if you can rustle up some breakfast for us?"

"I'll do that, but don't you leave this room," she cautioned.

As soon as she left, Layne sat down on the edge of the bed. A sharp pain was gripping his chest and he felt a thick numbness in his left arm. His face broke into a sweat as he reached for the tin in his pocket. He opened it, popped a nitro pill under his tongue and carefully placed the tin back in his pocket. He sat there for a few minutes while the blood flow and oxygen to his heart increased and the pain eased. He arose to his feet and walked into the bathroom.

No sooner had he closed the door than Michelle walked in with a tray containing their breakfast. "I've got breakfast for you."

From the bathroom, he called out as he turned on the shower, "I'll be a few. I'm just getting in the shower."

When he finished and dressed, he walked out of the bathroom, he sat and wolfed down his cold cereal as Michelle looked him over. He seemed to be more normal, but she still was worried.

When he finished breakfast and gathered the last of his belongings, they departed the motel room and headed for the truck and trailer.

"Grandpa," she called.

"What?"

"Aren't you forgetting something?"

Layne patted his face to make sure he had his glasses on. He checked his pocket and found his harmonica and keys, then looked at Michelle. "Like what?"

"You always check the oil before we start out," she reminded him.

"Oh yeah. What was I thinking?"

Upon checking the oil level, Layne remarked, "Great googly moogly. We need to add oil. Must have burned more than I thought in those mountains." He added the oil, then climbed into the truck. Then he drove up to the motel office and checked out. Afterward, they pulled into a nearby gas station where he filled up the tank and Michelle purchased coffees for them.

When she returned to the pickup truck and handed him his coffee, he gave her the AAA TripTik that he had been studying. "Here's the tick-tock. We've got about a five-hour drive to Chincoteague. We should be there by dinner time."

"Good," she commented. She sipped her coffee and he started the truck. She began studying the TripTik to help with the day's drive.

Two hours later, they were driving in traffic as they skirted around Baltimore. "I don't like all of this traffic," Layne muttered as he drove below the speed limit in the right lane.

"Looks like a parade behind us," Michelle laughed softly. She looked at her outside mirror and observed the line of vehicles that couldn't change lanes to drive around them.

Soon they were passing the outskirts of Annapolis and approaching the Chesapeake Bay Bridge at Sandy Point. The truck stopped at the toll booth and Layne paid the toll as a wide-eyed Michelle stared at the huge structure in front of them.

"That's bigger than the bridge over the Ohio River in Wheeling," she exclaimed in amazement.

"I read in the tick-tock this morning that it's over four miles long and one of the highest suspension bridges around," Layne commented.

"That thing is huge," Michelle said again as they drove onto the bridge. "This is scary, too." She readily saw how high they soon would be over the Chesapeake Bay.

"I bet winds up there could be pretty strong," Layne nodded to the highest point of the bridge.

Suddenly, Michelle turned to Layne and asked, "Grandpa, when we get to the other side, you're not going skinny-dipping like you did after we crossed the Ohio River, right?"

Layne chuckled. "Nothing to worry about. That is not on my bucket list."

After they crossed the bridge and drove along Route 50 on Kent Island, Layne said, "Michelle, keep your eye out for a gas station."

"But we just filled up."

"I need to use the bathroom, and maybe we'll top off the tank."

"There's one," she said as she spotted one in the distance.

Layne pulled in and parked next to one of the pumps. "I'll get her started and you can finish filling her while I go into the bathroom," he advised.

"Okay."

Michelle got out of the truck and joined him to pump gas. After getting it started, he went inside. When she finished, she walked around the trailer and checked on Irish Gin to ensure the horse was okay. She then walked to the front of the truck and leaned against it as she waited for Layne to return.

After ten minutes, she began to worry and decided to go inside the station to see where he was. As she approached it, she saw a movement to the east of the building in an adjacent parking lot. It was Layne. He was wandering up and down the parking aisles, trying to find the truck.

Michelle walked over to her grandfather. "Grandpa, are you looking for me?"

He turned with a befuddled look on his face. "Did you move

the truck?" I didn't know you could drive a stick shift," he said.

"No, Grandpa. It's out front by the gas pumps where you left us."

Layne looked past her at the pumps. "Of course. There we are," he said relieved. The two returned to the truck and headed on their way to Chincoteague.

When Layne noticed that Michelle had pulled out her cell phone and was keying in stuff, he asked her, "What are you doing?"

"Googling."

"What?"

"Googling. It's a search tool that I can use to access the internet and look up stuff," she explained.

"Great googly moogly! I was born before that internet. When I went to school, we didn't have to use that Google to learn stuff. We used the encyclopedia."

"This is faster. That's why I have a smart phone."

"A smart phone?" Layne crinkled his brow. "It's just a fad. Give it a couple of years. It'll go away. Just like that chia pet," he remarked, pleased that he remembered its name.

Michelle ignored him and focused on her cell phone.

As they drove, they listened to the radio. About thirty minutes out of Salisbury, a song by Charlie Roth began to play. It was called Grandpa's Little Girl.

> *Well that sure is a pretty flower*
> *but not half as pretty as your smile*
> *Wonder why they call em weeds*
> *We can blow the little seeds*
> *Watch em on the wind a while.*

What's that! Looks like you found a
feather I bet it's from a baby bird
Here's a little song we sing together
it's the sweetest one these ears have ever heard.

Grandpa's little girl! Grandpa's little girl
with her hand around my finger,
showing me the wonders of her world.

I bet you've never seen a spider,
there's a daddy long legs in the tree
walking on his web, jumping on his bed
like he's got a little trampoline.
We can watch the ants in the sandbox,
I can push you on the swing
made from a rope and tire.
You say let's go higher
that's when you start giggling.

Grandpa's little girl! Grandpa's little girl
with her hand around my finger,
wrapping me around her little finger
showing me the wonders of her world.

Well he sure is a lucky man,
you still have that pretty smile,
the church is full of flowers
and I recall those hours
as I watch you walk down the aisle.

You were Grandpa's little girl, Grandpa's little girl

with your hand around my finger,
wrapping me around your little finger.
He'll put a golden band around your finger
and you'll wander off into his world.

"I like that song," Layne smiled at his granddaughter. "It reminds me of you," he added warmly.

"I do, too. Grandpa. It sounds like the two of us." She gave her grandfather a sweet look. "I could listen to that song over and over."

"I could, too."

"I remember when we found that bird nest that had blown out of a tree. It had baby robins in it and you put it back in the tree."

"I remember," Layne smiled.

"And you built that tire swing for me so I could use it when I would come over with mom to visit before we moved in with you. Then you pushed me and I tried to touch the clouds with my toes," Michelle said, recalling a sweet moment of her childhood.

"And you almost touched them."

Michelle turned her head and gazed lovingly at Layne. "I guess I was really Grandpa's little girl, right?"

"You were, and you will always be no matter how old you get, Honey."

When they reached the other side of Salisbury, Layne reached into his pocket and withdrew his cell phone. "Can you find the phone number for your cousin for me and dial it. It's under Roeske." He then handed his cell phone to her. "Give it back to me after you dial it. And put it on speaker."

"Sure," she said. She quickly looked through his contacts and found Donna's number. Dialing it, she handed the phone back to Layne as Roeske answered.

"Zeke, are you here?" Roeske asked.

"We just went through Salisbury. We're on Route 13. It shouldn't be too much longer."

"I had to run to Accomac, but I should be back before sunset. I'll meet you at the marina so you two can see one of the best sunset views around," Roeske said. "You just go through town on Main Street and drive south. You'll see Captain Bob's Marina on the right."

"That sounds simple enough."

"Did you have supper yet?"

"Not yet. I was planning on stopping when we drove on the island."

"The firemen have the carnival open if you want to stop on your way. You'll drive right by it."

"Carnival? Yes. Let's stop there, Grandpa," Michelle said excitedly. She loved carnival fries and riding Ferris wheels.

Layne smiled. "We'll grab a bite there. Thanks for letting us know, Donna."

"No problem. I'll call you when I get to the marina so you can head down."

"Thanks, Donna," Layne said as they ended the call.

They continued driving south, entering Virginia.

"Grandpa."

"Yes?"

"I've been thinking."

"That's a good thing to do. What have you been thinking about?"

"Irish Gin."

"And?"

"She and I have become really good friends on this trip."

"I know. I realized that some time ago. Just waiting for you to realize it, Honey."

"I don't want to sell her to the Chincoteague firemen. I want to keep her."

"That makes me very happy."

"But I wasted your time in driving down here," Michelle sighed.

"Taking this trip with you is not a waste of time. It's a very special time to spend together. We'll sort out everything during our visit with Donna," he assured her.

"Thank you for understanding, Grandpa."

"That's what grandpas do best."

When they saw the sign for Chincoteague Island, they turned left on Route 175. They followed it past the NASA Visitor Center on Wallops Island onto the causeway through the marsh and across Blacks Narrows and Chincoteague Channel onto Chincoteague Island.

Michelle was relieved that their drive was coming to an end. There had been several harrowing moments when Layne misunderstood her directions and started to exit down the wrong ramps or would drift into the next lane. She had been on edge as she had to keep alert for his driving miscues.

When they drove onto the island, Layne turned to Michelle. "I want to make a stop before we go the carnival."

"Okay. Where are we going? I thought we were going to eat there."

"The cemetery. I want to say hello to your grandmother. First things first," he said as he drove to the cemetery. It had been years since he had been there.

When they arrived at the cemetery, he parked alongside the road and they exited the truck. In his hand, Layne carried the coffee cans that separately held the remains of Cathy and Sheba. Followed by Michelle, he walked directly to the tombstone inscribed with the name: Leona Layne. He then knelt on the ground and reverently rubbed the granite tombstone.

"I'm back sweetheart," he said in a loving tone. Tears welled up in his eyes. "I've missed you so much, my dear." He was silent for a while in quiet meditation. "I brought you company. I've got Cathy and Sheba here. I'll get them buried here with you," he said sadly as he rubbed the cold tombstone. "One day, all of us will be together again."

They stayed at the cemetery for fifteen minutes before returning to the truck. He gently placed the coffee cans in the truck's cab and they climbed inside.

"How about that carnival?" he asked Michelle. "Are you hungry?"

"I'm ready for some fries, Grandpa!"

They headed back to Main Street and drove south through the downtown filled with charming antique shops, art galleries, souvenir shops and restaurants.

"There's Misty!" Michelle said when she spied the statue of the horse made famous in the children's book *Misty of Chincoteague*. "I read that book!"

"Your mother bought that book for you," Layne recalled fondly.

They drove past a number of chain hotels and independent boutique hotels dotting the waterfront as well as many fishing piers.

"There's the carnival," Michelle said as she spotted the grounds on the left side of the road.

"Right you are. And there's parking across from the entrance for us," he said. He slowed and pulled into the bayfront parking lot. The two exited the vehicle and walked across the street to enter the grounds.

"What do you want to do first?"

"Fries!" she answered.

They spotted a carnival fry vendor and bought one order of fries which Michelle salted heavily.

"You want some, Grandpa?"

"I'll take a couple."

"What about you? Are you going to get something?"

Seeing a sign that announced home-cooked chili, Layne said, "I think I'll get a bowl of that chili."

After getting it, they walked around eating their food and checking out the rides, games of chance and other food vendors. They ended up buying elephant ears to munch on and later, lemonades to wash them down.

"Look Grandpa! If you break three balloons, you can win one of those stuffed ponies. That one looks like Irish Gin," she pointed eagerly.

"Want to try?"

"I'm no good at this stuff," she moaned.

"I think today is the start of a new adventure for you, Honey. Go ahead and try."

Layne paid the fireman for the three darts that Michelle picked up. She held one in her right hand and narrowed her eye as she aimed at her target. Cocking her hand back, she flung it forward, missing the balloon.

"Missed that one, Grandpa."

"Try again. This will just be a practice round."

She took her time before throwing the next two darts and broke one balloon. "Almost," she said.

Layne pulled another five dollars out of his wallet and handed it to the fireman. "Try again."

Michelle screwed up her face in a contorted look of concentration as she aimed at the balloons. Again, she broke only one balloon.

"I'm no good at this."

"I got a feeling in my bones that you'll connect on the next try." He pulled out a $20 bill and gave it to the fireman with a wink. "She'll take three more."

When the fireman started to give him change, Layne shook his head and winked at the fireman again. The fireman realized what Layne wanted to do and wasn't sure that he could help them out.

Michelle tried a different throwing position and leaned forward. "Is it okay if I lean in a little?" she asked the fireman.

"You can lean in a little, but don't over do it. It wouldn't be fair."

Michelle let fire with the first dart and it broke a balloon. "Yes!" she screamed as she jumped up and down.

"Two to go," Layne smiled. "I know you can do it."

Michelle took her time in lining up the second shot. She cocked back her wrist and let if fly. Pop! She broke another balloon.

"One more Grandpa and I have that horse that looks like Irish Gin," she said with wide eyes.

"You have a horse that looks like one of these?" the fireman asked. He pointed at the horses hanging from the ceiling.

"Yes. She looks like that palomino. My grandpa got her for me at your pony auction a few years ago."

"I see," he smiled. "Nothing like a Chincoteague pony."

Michelle nodded, then began to concentrate on breaking the third balloon. Her eyes narrowed as she aimed. She flicked her wrist forward, missing the balloon.

She turned to face her grandfather and before she could say anything, they heard a pop. She turned back and the balloon she had targeted had burst.

"Delayed reaction, I guess," the fireman said. He grinned as he reached overhead for the golden palomino and handed it to her.

"Cool beans!" She was thrilled as she hugged the pony tightly.

Layne looked at the fireman and mouthed "thank you." The fireman in return gave him a thumbs up.

"What do you want to do now?" Layne asked. "Donna hasn't called yet."

"Let's go on some rides."

"Which one first?"

"Ferris wheel," she said. She grabbed her grandfather's hand and led him to the Ferris wheel while gripping the stuffed horse in her other hand.

Layne bought tickets and they had a short wait before it was their turn to board.

"I counted 16 gondolas," Michelle said as she watched the wheel rotate with its rider-filled gondolas. While they waited, she turned to Layne. "Grandpa?"

"Yes?"

"I really enjoyed being with you on this trip. Thank you for loving me and making my life so special."

"I couldn't have made this trip without you. Who would have navigated for me and kept me going in the right direction?"

"You could have used that tick-tock as easily as I did," she countered using his words for a TripTik.

"I don't think so. Besides, it was nice seeing you and Irish Gin becoming friends again," he said. He leaned over and kissed her on the top of her head.

"Just like old times," she said with smiling eyes as she looked up at him.

"Almost like old times," he murmured.

Boarding the Ferris wheel, they sat in their gondola as it slowly made its way to the top while it unloaded and loaded riders.

"This is sort of like riding an elevator in a rocking chair," Layne suggested.

"It is," Michelle agreed. They edged up to the peak of the ride.

"Look at the view!" Michelle said excitedly. She turned around to enjoy the view and rocked their gondola.

"Easy there, Michelle. Don't tip us over," a nervous Layne cautioned.

"Sorry Grandpa. It's been so long since I've been on a Ferris wheel."

Layne pointed to the southwest side of the island. "See that marina over there?"

"Yes."

"That belongs to Donna. It's the biggest marina on the island."

"Cool beans," she said. The Ferris wheel began to move faster.

"This would be a nice ride at night. It'd make you feel like you could touch the stars."

"We could almost connect with Mom," Michelle said. She clutched her stuffed horse.

"Almost," Layne grinned.

When they disembarked, Michelle grabbed her grandfather's hand and led him toward the scrambler ride. "This one. Let's do this one."

"Okay," Layne said. He headed to buy tickets for them. He wasn't looking forward to another ride as he felt a case of heartburn coming on.

After he bought the tickets, they boarded one of the scrambler's cars. Once the ride started, they were spinning around like an egg beater. Layne felt like both his stomach and brain were getting scrambled like eggs as the ride's colorful arms swirled around in a rainbow of color.

When the ride ended, Layne turned to Michelle. "You're going to need to help me out of this."

Seeing his ashen gray face, she asked, "Are you feeling okay?"

"Yes. Just a little heartburn," he replied. She helped him step out of the car. When his feet hit the ground, he wobbled and had to reach for the side of the car to steady himself.

"You don't look good, Grandpa."

"I'll be fine. Just give me a moment."

The firefighter who was running the ride walked over to them. "Sir, are you all right?"

"It was the chili and getting tossed around in that ride," Layne explained. Michelle and the firefighter helped Layne walk out of the ride area to a nearby bench.

"You sit here and I'll be back to check on you," the firefighter advised. He left to load the next group of riders.

"Can I get you something to drink?" Michelle asked nervously.

Spotting a cold drink stand nearby, Layne pointed to it. "I could use a cola to help settle my stomach." He reached into his pocket and extracted his wallet. Giving her five dollars, he replaced his wallet in his pants pocket.

While she waited for her order to be filled, Michelle glanced nervously at her grandfather, then returned to his side with the cola. "Here you go."

Layne took the drink and slowly took a couple of gulps of the cold liquid. "That's much better." Although he still felt the discomfort, he didn't want to let Michelle know. "Let's just sit here for a few minutes and enjoy the sights and sounds of the carnival."

"Okay."

Within a few minutes, his cell phone rang and he answered it. It was Donna calling to tell them that she was at the marina.

"We'll be over in about ten minutes," Layne said. He ended the call, then turned toward Michelle. "Ready to go watch the sunset?"

"I'm ready," Michelle confirmed. She arose and helped him to his feet. She placed one arm within his. She noticed him looking around the carnival grounds. He had a confused look on his face. "Ready to go, Grandpa?"

"Which way to the parking lot?"

"This way, Grandpa," she said. She walked them through the grounds to the parking lot across the street.

"I'm just tired."

Layne didn't feel like himself, but he wasn't going to let on about it to his granddaughter. In fact, he felt a deep discomfort that was unfamiliar to him. Before getting into the truck, Layne gazed at the bay and the horizon.

"It's going to be a real pretty sunset tonight."

"I can't wait to see it!" she exclaimed.

He then climbed into the truck as did Michelle to begin the

short drive over to Capt. Bob's Marina. In another five minutes they pulled into the gravel parking lot of the marina where they immediately spotted Roeske standing by the edge of the bay. Layne drove over to her and parked.

"It's been a long time, Zeke," Donna said as she approached the truck.

"It has, Donna. I don't think you ever met Cathy's girl, Michelle."

"Hi Donna," Michelle said as she started to get out of the truck.

"Glad to meet you finally. Your mother was so dear to me. I'm so sorry about her passing away."

"Thank you."

Michelle walked over to give Roeske a big hug. She found an instant connection with Roeske and being with someone who once was so dear to her recently departed mother.

"You and I going to get along just fine," the blonde-haired woman said with a touch of a southern drawl. "Zeke, are you going to get out of that truck or do I have to drag you out?"

"I just might watch the sunset from here," he replied.

Turning to Roeske, Michelle explained, "He ate something at the carnival that doesn't agree with him."

"You want some Pepto Bismol or Tums, Zeke? I've got some in the marina."

"No. No. It will pass." Layne paused, then said, "Michelle, you might want to take Irish Gin out and let her stretch her legs a bit."

"That's a great idea. Come and meet my horse, Donna," Michelle offered. She then headed for the rear of the trailer.

Roeske followed her around and watched as she opened the bottom Dutch doors. As Michelle walked inside and led the horse out, Roeske asked, "You ride her a lot?" She stroked the back of the horse.

"No. She threw me a while back and I haven't been on her since."

"I'd say that horse loves you. I can tell. I have several of my own."

"She and I have grown a lot closer on this trip," Michelle acknowledged.

"Then what are you waiting for? Saddle her up. I see a saddle in there," Roeske urged.

"I don't know," Michelle said hesitantly.

"Come on. I'll give you a hand." Without waiting for a reply, Roeske walked into the trailer and grabbed the tack. When she walked out, she handed a blanket to Michelle. "Go ahead. Start saddling her. I'm not going to do this all by myself."

Michelle complied with her request and in a minute, they had Irish Gin ready to go.

"Up you go. Time's a-wasting. You do remember how to get on a horse, don't you?" Roeske pushed. She wasn't one to dilly dally around.

Holding the reins in one hand, Michelle moved to the side of the horse. Irish Gin turned her head and neighed as if to encourage her to mount her. Carefully, Michelle placed her left foot in the stirrup and boosted herself up. She swung her right leg over and put her foot in the other stirrup.

"Comfortable?" Roeske asked.

"Yes," she said nervously.

"That horse loves you, girl. Cut out that worried look on your face and ride her up next to the truck. Let your grandfather see you on her. I just know it will make his day," Roeske pushed.

Michelle clicked her tongue twice and guided the horse around the trailer and up to her grandfather's truck window.

"Look at me, Grandpa!" Michelle had a huge smile on her face.

Layne had seen them approaching in his outside mirror and beamed at her overcoming her fear. "See! Didn't I tell you that you'd be riding her one day. I even told you cross my heart, and hope to die."

"You did." Michelle was getting more comfortable from her perch. "She must know she's home."

"Maybe. That's why she's no longer out of sorts," Layne suggested.

"I guess none of us is out of sorts, right Grandpa?"

"That's probably right. Now you three go on over by the bay and watch the sunset. I'll watch it and you three from here."

"Don't you want to come with us?" Michelle asked.

"I can see you and the sunset just fine from here. It's been a long couple of days and I'm just going to relax here a spell."

"Okay," Michelle said as she, Irish Gin and Roeske headed to the water's edge.

The yellow ball of fire changed to hues of orange and then almost tangerine as it merged with the sky, dotted with clouds like cotton candy. Several seagulls flew across a sky that was now magenta, and the sun cast its reflection on Chincoteague Bay.

Layne's eyes were focused on the horizon, his face aglow with the last rays before dusk fell. His lips had a semblance of a smile, just enough to show that he was enjoying his thoughts.

Since the ride on the scrambler, Layne had tried to hide the pain he felt in his chest, but now it was growing. It was more intense and he could feel the tightness. He reached inside his pocket and withdrew the tin of nitro. Opening it, he started to take one out, but then stopped. Instead, he closed the tin and returned it to his pocket.

His eyes began to drift to rest as a calmness flew by with the wind. He could hear the grasses rustling as if they were whispering to him, "Come home, Zeke. Come home."

Time to join his wife Leona, Cathy and Sheba, he thought as he looked through partially open eyes. As the sun set on the horizon so did Layne's eyes set. They would not open again as he took his last breath. He was content.

As dusk appeared, Michelle rode Irish Gin over to the truck. "Wasn't that beautiful, Grandpa?" she asked. Seeing his closed eyes, she turned to Roeske who had walked up next to her. "I think he fell asleep. Poor guy. It's been a long three days."

Roeske took a quick look. "Let him sleep for a few minutes while we put your horse back in the trailer. Then we need to get over to my place and put your horse up for the night and get you two some good dinner."

The three went to the rear of the trailer and took off the tack. Michelle led Irish Gin into the trailer. When they closed up the Dutch doors, they walked back to Layne's side of the truck.

"Zeke, wake up! We need to get over to my place," Roeske called. When he didn't respond, she turned to Michelle. "He must be in a really deep sleep. I'll shake him awake."

Michelle nodded and watched as Roeske opened the truck door and shook Layne. He toppled over, lifeless. Roeske realized that Layne had passed away. She turned to Michelle and placed her arm around her to comfort her. "Sweetie, your grandfather has gone to be with your mother," she said as she softly consoled Michelle.

"He's no longer out of sorts," Michelle sobbed at her loss.

EPILOGUE

Over the next few days there was a flurry of activity as preparations were made for Layne's funeral in Chincoteague. Michelle told Roeske that she wasn't going to invite Blair or Ida. She then told her everything that had happened starting with the recent death of her mother through their arrival on Chincoteague Island.

Roeske was stunned to hear the dreadful tale and invited Michelle to live with her permanently. Michelle quickly agreed as it put distance between her and Blair and Ida.

While they were going through Layne's suitcase, they found the envelope that Layne had placed inside it after their stop in west Akron. The envelope was addressed to Michelle. She opened it and found a note.

Dear Michelle,

If you're reading this, it means that I've
gone to be with your grandmother, mother
and Sheba. I don't want you to be sad. It's
a good thing for me and at the right time.

I want you to know how much I love you
and that the four of us will be looking down
upon you whenever you look up at the
stars. We will be sending you our love.

*I want you to call Randal Lowry. His business
card is in my wallet. He's the lawyer we met
at the ferry dock. I helped him jump his
Porsche. He has some things to tell you.*

*I will always love you and Irish Gin –
Cross my heart, and hope to die. You
will always be Grandpa's little girl.*

Love,

Grandpa

With a perplexed look on her face, Michelle opened Layne's wallet and found Lowry's business card with his phone number. She grabbed her cell phone and called him.

"Mr. Lowry, this is Michelle, Zeke Layne's granddaughter. We met at the Miller Ferry dock. He helped you start your car."

"I remember you, Michelle," Lowry responded.

"I had a note from my grandfather to call you when he passed away. He died yesterday after we got to Chincoteague Island," she explained.

"I am so sorry, Michelle. Although I knew him briefly, he seemed like such a fine man. Very likeable," Lowry said in a caring tone. "Are you okay? Are you with family?"

"Yes. I'm with my cousin and it looks like I'll be moving in with her. She has several horses and a small ranch here."

"Good. I'm glad to hear that. The reason Zeke wanted you to contact me was to let you know that he met with me at the beginning of your trip."

"That's why we stopped in Akron!" Michelle exclaimed.

She recognized the address for his office.

"He had called me that morning and asked me to prepare a new will for him. He stopped by to sign it and to write that note to you."

"What does that mean?" Michelle asked.

"Was he concerned with the two stepdaughters?"

"Yes. They were always after his money and they were going to put him in a nursing home and make me move in with them," she said quickly.

"I don't believe that they will be an issue any longer. His new will makes you the sole beneficiary. How old are you?"

Michelle didn't respond right away. She was stunned by the revelation. "I'm seventeen, but I turn eighteen in two weeks."

"Good. That makes things simpler since you will be emancipated."

"I don't understand," Michelle said, confused. "I don't know what all I have to do."

"Let me put your mind at ease and I'll do most of the work for you." Lowry explained the process that they would go through, including the disposition of the mobile home and any assets and the transfer of Layne's savings.

After they had discussed it, Lowry asked, "Do you have any questions?"

"One."

"Yes?"

"Who is going to tell Blair and Ida? I bet they're going through everything at the mobile home now."

"Would you like me to?" Lowry asked.

"Yes." Michelle gave him Blair's cell phone number and the number for the Catawba police chief, Ryan Sigler.

"I will take care of everything and I'll call you once it's

done."

They ended the call and Lowry called Sigler. Thirty minutes later, Sigler parked his SUV next to Blair's car at Layne's mobile home. He exited the vehicle and walked into the mobile home. He was stunned by what he saw. It was a disaster. Furniture had been cut apart as if someone was trying to find something of value hidden away.

"Oh Blair, look it's that policeman who helped us at the Holiday Inn Express."

"The police chief," Sigler corrected her as the two women walked into the living room.

"What can we do for you?" Blair asked. She looked sweaty and disheveled from tearing up the contents of the mobile home.

"Leave." Sigler said. He didn't like either woman and was aware of how they had treated Layne.

"Why?" Ida asked.

"You may not know that Zeke passed away," Sigler said stoically.

"He did!" Blair exclaimed with relief.

"He's dead! Is he really dead?" Goofball Ida could barely contain her glee at the thought of getting their hands on Layne's savings much easier than what they had thought.

"Yes. I'm sorry to say."

"We don't have to leave. We are the heirs. I've a copy of the will," Blair spat the words out defiantly.

"I've got Zeke's lawyer, Randal Lowry on my cell phone. It's on speaker," Sigler said. He held up the phone and the two stepsisters stared at it with a lack of comprehension.

"Ladies, I'd like to inform you that Mr. Layne drew up a new will and you are not included as a beneficiary. As such, the sole beneficiary would like you to vacate the premises and Chief

Sigler is here to enforce our request."

"You can't do that. He couldn't have changed the will" a shocked Blair retorted.

"Yeah. We have the final will," Ida added with a wild-eyed look.

Sigler wasn't one for wasting time in arguing. He stepped behind the women and starting gently pushing them towards the door. Reluctantly they complied, but went screaming and shouting to their car. They were still screaming as they drove away.

Lowry thanked Sigler and called Michelle to let her know what had transpired.

The next evening, a funeral service was held for Layne. Several people from the Catawba area drove or flew down to Chincoteague including the Markets, Matthew Parker, Kenny Kartheiser, Kim Bartish, and Jerry and Cathy Davenport, who picked up their horse trailer and took it back to Ohio after the funeral.

Layne's body was cremated. His ashes were buried with Cathy and Sheba's ashes next to Leona at the cemetery in Chincoteague. That evening when the Miller Ferry left the Catawba Dock for its final run of the day, it gave the Master's Salute in farewell to Zeke Layne – three long blasts followed by two short blasts of its horn.

Michelle worked with Lowry to wrap up the estate and transfer her grandfather's savings to a Chincoteague bank. She also donated their Catawba mobile home to the Miller Ferry Line to do with as they wished. She had no intentions of returning to Catawba since her true family were buried on Chincoteague.

She enrolled in Chincoteague High School and fell in love

with a classmate, Ryan Terry, who also had a horse and played the harmonica. Michelle gave him Layne's harmonica and he was thrilled. They were married shortly after graduation and built a home on Roeske's ranch.

Terry was skilled in auto body repair and did an off-the-frame restoration of Layne's truck, including fixing the rusted-out floor. Michelle was excited to see how good the truck looked and even more excited when Terry taught her how to drive a stick shift.

Many nights they would ride to Captain Bob's Marina to watch the sun fall behind the horizon, painting the sky shades of red and pink. As dusk turned into night, Terry would play the harmonica. They would watch for the stars to shine, knowing that her family was shining love on them.

Some nights, they'd ride over to the cemetery and spend time at the family gravesite. Michelle would always smile when she looked at the quote below her grandfather's name on the tombstone. It read: Cross my heart and hope to die.

Coming Soon
The Next *Emerson Moore* Adventure
Sunset Blues